SAXBY
SCHOOLBOY DETECTIVE
SMART

D0714963

THE EYE OF THE SERPENT

SIMON CHESHIRE

Piccadilly

First published in Great Britain in 2009
by Piccadilly Press,
A Templar/Bonnier publishing company
Deepdene Lodge, Deepdene Avenue,
Dorking, Surrey, RH5 4AT
www.piccadillypress.co.uk

A catalogue record for this book is available
from the British Library

ISBN: 978 1 84812 008 2 (paperback)

1 3 5 7 9 10 8 6 4 2

Printed in the UK by CPI Group (UK), Croydon, CR0 4YY

The *Saxby Smart – Schoolboy Detective* series:
The Curse of the Ancient Mask
The Fangs of the Dragon
The Pirate's Blood
The Hangman's Lair
The Eye of the Serpent
Five Seconds to Doomsday
The Poisoned Arrow
Secret of the Skull

www.saxbysmart.co.uk

Eye
of the
Serpent

Introduction:
Important Facts

My name is Saxby Smart and I'm a private detective. I go to St Egbert's School, my office is in the garden shed, and this is a collection of my case files. Unlike some detectives, I don't have a sidekick, so that part I'm leaving up to you – pay attention, I'll ask questions.

CHAPTER ONE

THERE ARE SOME THINGS I'M quite good at. Such as, 1) being a brilliant schoolboy detective, and 2) keeping clear, detailed notes on my various detective-type investigations.

There are other things I'm not good at. Such as . . . well, pretty much everything else, really. I'm OK at schoolwork (except maths, eurgh, splutter, help), but the minute I try to do anything practical I go to pieces. I can't even open a tin of beans without covering half the kitchen with that orangey bean-juice.

So why did I think I could reorganise the garden shed, to make more space for my Crime HQ? Why? *Whyyyyy?* Because I never admit to myself that I can't do these things until it's too late, that's why.

You know how, sometimes, you'll be clearing out a drawer or a cupboard and you'll think to yourself: How did all of *this* fit inside of *that*? I was having exactly the same problem with the garden shed. The previous weekend I'd emptied the entire shed out on to the lawn and tried to put it all back in the most space-saving way possible. And I'd ended up more cramped up in there than ever before.

Now Saturday had come around again and I was having another go. On to one side of the lawn I dragged all my essential detective gear: my desk, my filing cabinet full of case notes and my battered old leather Thinking Chair. On to the other side of the lawn, I dragged all the piles of stuff I'm forced to share the shed with: the lawnmower, the garden hose, assorted gardening-type kit, half-empty paint pots, boxes of DIY equipment and tons of other heavy, grubby old tat.

Right, I thought to myself, this is just a simple problem of organisation. Like those video games where you have to slot shapes in on top of each other.

Two hours later I'd packed everything back into the shed. Including myself. I sat in my Thinking Chair and I looked up at the enormous pile I'd jammed in on the other side of my desk and I thought to myself: That's all going to fall over in a minute and I'm going to be buried under the lawnmower.

Oooohhh, whyyyyyy did I ever start this?

I hardly dared move. I'd got my desk sorted out, and my case files, and my chair. But everything else was now teetering overhead in a kind of looming wall. One good sneeze and the lot would come down.

I let out a long, weary sigh. 'I'm going to have to start all over again, aren't I?' I muttered to myself.

Suddenly, there was a knock at the shed door. The looming wall of stuff wobbled. That might have been caused by the knocking or it might have been caused by the way I nearly jumped out of my skin.

'Come in,' I called. 'Carefully.'

James Russell, my old friend from school, clomped into the shed. You might remember him if you've read my case file, *The Pirate's Blood*. Quiet, serious guy, pointy face, dollop of curly hair.

'H'lo Saxby,' he said. 'Have you been redecorating in here?'

'Er, something like that,' I said, keeping a nervous eye on the wobbling stack beside me.

'I need your help,' said James.

He sat in my Thinking Chair while I hopped up on to the desk. I sat back, gently leaning against the tottering boxes to try to keep them stable.

'What's the problem?' I asked.

James gave a tiny little, throat-clearing 'ahem', fist

5

poised at his lips. 'Well,' he said, 'last time I came to see you, I had a tale of blood-chilling horror to relate.'

'Mm-hmm,' I agreed, nodding.

'This time,' he said, his voice shuddering slightly, 'I have a tale of nerve-tingling fear!'

'Excellent,' I said, rubbing my hands together in glee. The stuff behind me wobbled again. I decided to stay still.

'Do you believe in bad luck, Saxby? Do you believe that an object can carry bad luck around with it? Do you believe that something can be evil and bring misfortune to all who touch it?'

'No,' I said.

James's eyes went a little bit boggly. 'You might change your mind when you hear what's happened.'

I leaned forward, frowning. The stack behind me creaked. 'What's happened?' I said quietly.

'Last night,' said James, even more quietly, 'I saw the Eye of the Serpent vanish before my very eyes!'

'The what of the what?' I asked.

'The Eye of the Serpent,' said James, in a trembly voice. 'I was watching it and it literally vanished into thin air!'

I was confused. 'Was this in a zoo or something?'

'No, the new art gallery in Gladstone Road.'

I was more confused. 'What was a snake doing in the

art gallery? Admiring the paintings?'

'Huh? Nooooo, the Eye of the Serpent is a statuette. It was a piece of artwork on display.'

'Ooooooooh, riiiight,' I said, rolling my eyes a little. 'Start again. Tell me exactly what happened, from the beginning.'

'OK,' said James, taking a deep breath. 'As you know, my dad runs the local museum. He's friends with this guy who's just set up a new art gallery in Gladstone Road. It's in that building that used to be the library before the library moved. You know?'

'Er, yes, I think so,' I said. 'All stone pillars and high ceilings?'

'That's the place. Anyway, my dad knows this guy because they both have the same boss at the Department of Dusty Old Relics or whatever it's called. The gallery has taken ages to set up, and it opened for the first time last night. There was a formal party there, invited guests only. You know the sort of thing: posh outfits, polite chitchat, snooty attitudes.'

'Sounds like a non-stop festival of laughs,' I said with the heaviest sarcasm I could manage.

'My dad made me help his friend out,' said James, pulling a grumpy face. 'I was gliding around all night with trays of celery nibbles. I had to wear a white shirt, bow tie, the lot.'

'You in a bow tie? Ha-haaaa!' I snorted.

'Pack it in,' said James. 'This gallery has got lots of things in it – paintings, pottery and so on – but it's opening with a special exhibition of Art Deco pieces.'

'What's Art Dekker?'

'Dec-*o*,' said James. 'Dunno, really, I'm not into that sort of thing. It's a kind of arty-style, full of women in floaty dresses who appear to be standing in a strong wind. There are lots of glass ornaments in this exhibition and framed pictures of people from eighty-odd years ago looking a bit miserable. There's even clothes and lamp stands and everyday objects.'

'And you say this Eye of the Serpent is a small statue?' I said.

'A statuette, yes,' said James. 'It's about thirty centimetres high, and jet black. It looks like a rearing cobra, sideways-on, and there's a ruby where its eye should be. It's an evil-looking thing – it gives me the creeps.'

'Is it valuable?' I said.

'Are you kidding? I found out last night it's worth two million pounds!'

I almost fell off the desk. The mountain of boxes behind me creaked alarmingly again. 'Wow!' I mouthed. 'A creepy little thing like that?'

James shuffled forward on the Thinking Chair. His

voice dropped to a whisper. 'The gallery manager's assistant was telling me all about it. It's so valuable because it's one of the few surviving pieces by Enid Bottomby, almost the greatest artist of the twentieth century.'

'Why "almost"?'

'Because,' whispered James, 'it's said that her life was cursed, full of tragic happenings and other doom-type events. Arty people who know about these things say that she should be one of the most famous names in modern art but her work has mostly been lost and she's been mostly forgotten. There are only a dozen known Bottombys left in the world.'

'And this Eye of the Serpent is one of them,' I said.

'Right,' said James. 'Each of these pieces is said to bring bad luck to whoever possesses it. If the rest of her work is as scary as that statuette, I can well believe it!'

'So, naturally, you were watching it like a hawk last night,' I said. 'I mean, knowing you, you were expecting it to start emitting an eerie glow or something.'

'Exactly!' said James. 'You can't be too careful when there're supernatural forces about!'

I groaned to myself. 'James, I can promise you, if that statuette has gone missing then it's a simple case of theft, and —'

James suddenly bristled like a startled hedgehog.

'You weren't there!' he cried indignantly. 'I'm telling you, it simply *vanished*! Of course, there was uproar when I pointed out that it had gone. I jumped up and I shouted, 'Look, everyone! The Bottomby's gone!' Then the gallery manager started yelling about thieves. All the guests started yelling about thieves. An art critic from one of the newspapers fainted with shock.'

Then his eyes went so boggly I was worried for a moment that they might plop out on to the floor. 'Hey, maybe that's why so much of Enid Bottomby's artwork has been lost over the years? Maybe more of it vanished into thin air?'

I groaned to myself again. 'For goodness' sake, things don't just disappear like that. There has to be a logical explanation for what happened. And the chances are the logical explanation involves a thief, like all those people were yelling about.'

'But nobody could just have taken it.'

'Why not?'

'Because it was behind a brand new, high-power laser beam security net, that's why,' said James, very seriously. 'I promise you, no thief came anywhere near that statuette. I was *watching* it. It vanished into thin air before my eyes! The curse of Enid Bottomby has struck again!'

CHAPTER TWO

I HMMM-ED AND AHHH-ED FOR A BIT.

'OK,' I said at last, 'let's take this one step at a time. Step one: tell me exactly where this Eye of the Serpent was when it, er . . . vanished into thin air before your eyes.'

James stared at the shed floor and chewed at his lower lip as he visualised the scene. 'As you know, the gallery is in an old building. The room which houses the Art Deco exhibition is very large, and shaped like a rectangle. The ceiling is high and sort of curved at the top. There are tall windows at one end, and all around the walls there's a row of alcoves.'

'What, you mean, like recesses? Little areas that are kind of sunk into the wall?'

'Exactly, yes,' said James. 'They're not very big, about a metre and a half off the floor. They've been there since the place was built, apparently. There are about twenty of them in all. They're ideal for displaying small pieces of art – statuettes, china figures, that sort of thing. The Eye of the Serpent was placed in one of these alcoves, in the middle of the wall opposite the windows.'

'Was it the only thing on display in that particular alcove?' I asked.

'Oh, yes, there's really only room for one thing in each. There are a series of suspended lights in the room, and one of them was pointing directly at that alcove. The Eye of the Serpent was in a clear pool of light. You could see it from most parts of the room.'

'Tell me more about this brand new, high-power laser beam security net thingummy,' I said.

'It's really clever. There are different devices used for different parts of different displays, but they all work by projecting a criss-cross of invisible beams. Around the walls of the Art Deco room, there are strips in the floor, which project a tight net of lasers right across each wall from one side to the other. The net is about two centimetres away from the actual wall itself.'

'So people can go right up to the things on display but if they try to actually touch them then a whopping great *whah-whah-whah* starts up.'

'That's right,' said James. 'It's really cool, you can't see the beams or anything. This system cost a fortune to install.'

'Pity it's no bloomin' good then,' I grumbled.

'Huh?'

'Well, the system's not exactly good value for money, is it, if the gallery's pride and joy gets nicked on opening night.'

James pulled an ah-yes-that's-awkward face. 'Yeah, I see what you mean. But it proves my point, doesn't it? No thief took that statuette. They couldn't. If anything had broken those beams, the alarm would have sounded.'

'The alarm system was actually on, was it?'

'I know it was,' said James. 'When I was preparing trays of celery nibbles in the gallery's office I saw the manager's assistant switch the whole system on. Little flashing red lights, the works. All systems go.'

I frowned, rubbing my chin in a thoughtful and detectivey way. I had to admit, this case was starting to sound more and more puzzling.

'Could someone have reached the Eye of the Serpent some other way?' I wondered.

'Not possible,' said James, shaking his head. 'The entire wall was covered by the laser net. And nobody could have broken through the wall from the back. For one thing, everyone would have seen the hole! The alcove was untouched. The statuette simply disappeared from it.'

I frowned some more. 'And where precisely did you see the, er . . . disappearance from?'

'I was just having a rest from gliding around with trays of celery nibbles. There are these sort of padded benches dotted around the room and I was sitting on one close to the windows, on the opposite side of the room to the statuette.'

'But you could see the alcove clearly?'

'Yes. Like I said, I was keeping a sharp watch on the Eye of the Serpent, after what I'd heard about it.'

I frowned hard enough to make my face look as crumpled as the school uniform scattered across my bedroom floor. 'Now think carefully. You actually *saw* it vanish, did you?'

James shrugged. 'Weeeeell, obviously I wasn't sitting there literally not taking my eyes off it. I was looking around the room a bit too. I remember someone asked me for another celery nibble. And the manager's assistant slipped over on a puddle of wine someone had spilled and went down with an almighty crash. Which made me laugh. And of course I had to blink now and again! But I can't have taken my eyes off that alcove for more than a couple of seconds at a time. One second it was there and two or three seconds later, it wasn't. I tell you, it *vanished*.'

'And then you jumped up and yelled?'

'Yes.'

'And then there was general confusion?'

'Yes.'

There was a chilly sensation starting to creep along my spine. And it had nothing to do with the teetering pile of shed-debris that was still looming up behind me. If what James had told me was accurate – and I had no reason to doubt him – then here was a daring robbery, which had been carried out in the blink of an eye! Not only that, but a daring robbery which had somehow fooled a brand new, high-power laser beam security net thingummy! And not only *that*, but a daring robbery which had been carried out right in front of a room full of people!

'Well,' I said, trying to sound confident, 'whatever happened to the Eye of the Serpent, I can promise you that there were no supernatural forces involved. Not one tiny, weeny, microscopic little supernatural force of any kind. How many guests attended last night?'

'Ah, I know that exactly,' said James. 'Seventy-seven. At the start I had to collect up the invitations.'

'And they all had invitations? There was nobody who brought a couple of extra, uninvited friends with them?

No hangers-on?'

'Not as far as I could see,' said James. 'Like I said, they were a pretty posh bunch. They all seemed rather snobby and proud of the fact that they all had these printed card invites they could hand me.'

'Which means,' I said, more to myself than to James, 'that at least we can be sure who was there. There were a lot of them, but we know their names.'

Several possibilities were beginning to solidify in my mind, rather like school custard if you leave it standing on your dinner tray too long. This case was already worryingly baffling, but at this point three questions occurred to me. Three questions I should ask James, all of them relating directly to the guests.

Can you guess what I wanted to know?

Question No 1: Did you see anyone amongst the guests who looked suspicious?

James thought carefully. 'No, not at all. Several of them I'd seen before because they know my dad. Most of them were strangers to me but I didn't see anyone who looked shifty or who did anything odd. They were a pretty dull and over-serious crowd to be perfectly honest. Most of them seemed to spend the evening guzzling the free nibbles and wine and seeing who could boast the loudest about how much they knew on the subject of art.'

Question No 2: Did anyone else see the statuette vanish?

'No.'

'Really? Are you sure?'

'Yes.'

'Ah, so someone *did* see something?'

'No, I mean I'm sure they *didn't*.'

'Oh . . . right. I knew that.'

This struck me as very strange. Here were seventy-seven guests, plus gallery staff, plus James, and only James saw that the statuette had suddenly gone missing.

'Doesn't that strike you as strange?' I said.

'Well, now I come to think about it, yes,' said James. 'I suppose it does.'

'So, you raised the alarm,' I said, 'and nobody else could confirm that they'd seen the statuette disappear?'

'Nope.'

'That's very strange,' I muttered. 'There it was, the Eye of the Serpent, a really important part of the exhibition, and it gets stolen at precisely the moment when nobody is looking at it. Possibly the *only* moment when nobody is looking at it.'

James started chewing at his lip again, an expression of fear slowly sliding over his face like a slug sliding on wet leaves. 'And you're still telling me there's nothing supernatural about all this?' he trembled. 'Stolen at such a precise moment? What are the chances of *that* happening? I bet the Eye of the Serpent spotted that nobody was looking at it, saw its chance and did a runner into another dimension or something.'

'Oh, pack it in,' I grumbled. 'Wasn't there even anyone standing next to it?'

'Not at that exact minute, no. There were about half a dozen guests a couple of metres away, I think. The gallery manager was giving them catalogues.'

'Catalogues?' I said, puzzled. 'What, you mean like home-shopping catalogues?'

'Nooooo, the catalogue of items in the exhibition. A sort of guidebook to what's on display. Well, more a leaflet, really. Well, more a fold-out, kind of —'

'Yeah yeah yeah, I get the picture,' I said.

It suddenly occurred to me that I hadn't asked

Question No 3 yet. A-ha! The answer to this question would definitely shed some light on the matter! Definitely, definitely!

Question No 3: What happened when the police turned up and questioned the guests?

'They didn't,' said James. 'The guests were all so shocked at what had happened that they were sent home. Then I went home. I think the police turned up later.'

So, no light shed on the matter whatsoever . . .

'You've got to be kidding,' I gasped. I shut my eyes and let out a long sigh. 'Obviously, I didn't expect you to tell me that the guests were searched and the statuette was found in somebody's handbag. Obviously. Otherwise, you wouldn't have needed to come to me in the first place. But are you really telling me that every last witness to the crime just went home? Without being asked a single question? By anyone?'

''Fraid so,' shrugged James.

'The police *were* actually called, were they?' I said.

'Oh yes,' said James. 'The gallery manager said he'd do it as soon as his panic attack had eased off a bit.'

'Is that man an idiot?' I spluttered. 'Why didn't he stop the guests?'

'Be fair, he wasn't thinking straight,' said James. 'The poor man was in a right flap. His prize exhibit was gone.

From what I heard, he'd spent a year persuading the statuette's owner to let the gallery borrow it. That owner must be furious.'

'So am I!' I cried. 'What a twit! If there was a book called *The Rules of Detective Work*, then Rule 1 would be Don't Let All Your Suspects Go Home!'

'But he's not a detective, for goodness' sake,' said James. 'He runs an art gallery. The shock turned him into a nervous wreck. He was looking quite tearful by the time I went home.'

'But don't you see what this means?' I cried. I started bouncing up and down on the desk in frustration. But then the heaving mountain of stuff behind me started wobbling again. So I stopped. '*Someone* in that room stole the Eye of the Serpent. And if everyone just went home, then this whoever-it-is has got clean away with it! That statuette could be halfway to Peru or something by now!'

'Er, yes, well,' said James. 'Never mind, you're a brilliant schoolboy detective. You'll soon be hot on the trail of the culprit, right?'

I felt completely lost. It seemed like I had nothing to base my investigation on, no clues from which I could form any kind of theory. I felt like whimpering, 'Help.' Instead, I said, 'Er, yeah, right. I guess the first step is for me to visit the gallery and take a look at the scene of the crime.'

'Come over later today,' said James. 'I've been roped into helping out again. The gallery manager is holding a press conference and I'm helping do the seating. He's going to ask the media to launch a huge public search.'

'A fat lot of good that'll do,' I muttered under my breath. 'By the way,' I said, 'what did your dad make of all this?'

'Oh, he wasn't actually there last night,' said James. 'He was really busy – it's late-night opening at the museum on a Friday these days.'

'Late-night opening?' I said, amazed. 'I thought your museum struggled to get half a dozen visitors a week?'

'It did,' said James. 'But ever since you solved that Pirate's Blood mystery, we've had loads of people coming to see where those robbers planned their raid. We're on the tourist map these days – my dad's delighted.'

'Good grief,' I mumbled to myself.

'I'll see you later then,' said James, standing up and opening the shed door. 'Be there by about four.'

'OK,' I said, reaching across for my notebook. 'Mind you don't slam the —'

Whump!

As soon as the door slammed shut behind James, the heap of junk behind me started creaking forwards. I barely had time to scurry out of the way before a stack of plastic plant pots clattered on to the desk, spraying dried mud all over the place. The plant pots were followed by the lawnmower, which crashed down with its electrical cable unravelling like excited spaghetti.

I sat there, grumpy, watching the dust settle as it swirled in the light coming through the shed's perspex window. I was going to have to start this tidying-up thing all over again.

No time for any of that now. Thank goodness.

A Page From My Notebook

Observation: This must be the most peculiar case I've ever come across. HOW can you steal something that's brightly lit, in front of a roomful of people, from behind a security net? I can see WHY - it's very valuable - but the total mystery is HOW!

Other observation: I have at least seventy-seven suspects. This is not good. I get into enough confusion dealing with two or three!

Also, the police will now be talking to those seventy-seven guests well out of earshot of ME. I have no access to anything the police get up to. I'll have no way of investigating the guests. (Well, I COULD get the guest list from James, and go to see each of them one by one. But that would take weeks. And I don't think this case will wait weeks to get solved.)

Other, other observation: The gallery manager's assistant was the one who told James about the Bottomby curse. Can this person be trusted? SUDDEN THOUGHT: Does this person have a reason for wanting people to believe in a curse?

Possibility 1: Is the Eye of the Serpent all it seems? If pieces by Enid Bottomby are so rare and so shrouded in stories, could there be something about the statuette ITSELF that I don't know about yet?

Possibility 2: Should I take what I've heard at

face value? Surely the security system MUST have been tampered with, somehow? Otherwise, the theft really DOES seem impossible.

Possibility 3: ~~Could the celery nibbles have been secretly drugged, so that everyone fell asleep without knowing it and then~~ . . . No, forget that one. It's silly.

My Plan of Action: Keep a close eye on everything this afternoon, including the exhibit room, the security system, the gallery staff, the entrances and exits (through which the thief might have escaped), the . . . Oh, just EVERYTHING, OK?

CHAPTER THREE

BEFORE GOING TO THE ART GALLERY, I went to see my great friend George 'Muddy' Whitehouse. He's St Egbert's School's resident Mr Fixit. Anything you need that's mechanical or electronic, see Muddy.

He was busy in his garage – or Development Laboratory, as he prefers to call it – working on ways to add a games console to a bicycle. So far he'd managed to link a video display to his cycling helmet and was now assembling housing for the console just above the front wheel.

'It's a kind of in-flight entertainment system,' he said, sorting through some spanners.

'Surely,' I said, 'playing games and cycling at the same time is extremely dangerous?'

He thought for a moment or two. 'Hmm,' he said quietly, tapping a spanner against his oil-stained chin. 'You know, you may possibly have spotted a slight flaw in my idea.'

Once he'd put his bike back to normal, I explained why I'd come to see him. I asked him if he had anything which might help me. (You'll see what I mean in a page or two!)

'Ah,' he cried, one finger suddenly pointing at the ceiling. 'You'll want the Whitehouse C-Anything Ultra-Vision Spex! I made them using some night-vision binoculars, the circuits from a video camera and a pair of my mum's glasses. She needed some new ones anyway, these are hideous.'

I promised to return them safe and sound, then headed off to the gallery. It was about three forty-five p.m. when I arrived there, and the line of trees outside was swaying and hissing in the wind.

The gallery was a broad, sandy-coloured stone building. It had an immense, arched entrance into which had been fitted a revolving door made of thick, smoke-dark glass.

Inside, the place had surprisingly little natural light. I say 'surprisingly' because there was no shortage of windows. It was as if the walls inside the building didn't like being caught in daylight, and rudely pushed any stray sunbeams out of the way. Instead of light from the windows, everywhere was lit up with spotlights and large glowing domes, which gave the gallery an odd, almost spooky atmosphere.

The floors were a gleaming pattern of black and white tiles. My shoes klumped loudly as I followed signs which pointed the way to *The Art Deco Experience*. Stuck beneath each sign was a neatly printed sheet which said: *Temporary Closure Due to Major Crime Incident. Re-opens Monday. Tickets Available at Gallery Entrance and online.*

I wrinkled my nose up. I hadn't realised that this exhibition was one of those attractions that charges you extra to go and see the one thing you came to see in the first place. If you see what I mean. That sort of thing really annoys me.

I walked through several long rooms lined with paintings and dotted with old pots on plinths. There were quite a few visitors, wandering around in silent slow motion as if the paintings would fall off the walls in fright if someone so much as coughed. Most of them seemed to be grumbling about the fact that the Art Deco Experience was shut today.

At last I came to a large partition with double doors in the middle of it, all made out of the same smoky-looking glass as the revolving door at the entrance. A large board with swirly, intricate lettering announced the exhibition.

The double doors were shut so I tapped hesitantly at them, the smoky glass making the room beyond look like a haze of thick, grey fog. Two figures emerged from the fog, their outlines shimmering. As they got closer, one turned out to be James and the other was a young woman in a smart trouser suit. She was carrying an armful of papers which looked like they'd spill out of control at any moment, and she kept hooking her long dark hair around the back of her ears. Balancing the papers on one arm, she unlocked the doors and ushered me inside.

'Hi! Saxby?' she said in a posh accent, slightly out of breath.

'That's me,' I said with a grin.

'Great. OK. Must dash. Catch you later,' she said, scuttering away. 'Oh,' she gasped, turning a full circle in mid-step, 'I'm Davina. Hello! Sorry.'

'Looks like she's in a hurry,' I said to James.

'She's always in a hurry,' replied James.

The exhibition room was exactly as James had described it. So I won't bother telling you all about it again. The only thing he hadn't mentioned was that the floor space was neatly arranged with various displays too. Statues and glassware sat on tall, round stands with elegantly printed information notices positioned beside them. Images of artists and reproductions of old photos were set alongside paintings, ornaments, and even a couple of designer chairs.

'This looks *really* good,' I said. My voice echoed slightly against the high ceiling and the shiny, highly polished tiled floor.

'Davina designed it all,' said James. 'They've got some fabulous gear in the office. I'll show you in a minute.'

'First things first,' I said. 'Let's take a look at the Eye of the Serpent. Or rather, the gap where the Eye of the Serpent used to be.'

James led me across the room, weaving around the display stands. I looked about me, trying to picture the scene from last night.

The alcove in which the statuette had been placed was the middle one of seven, which were evenly spaced along the length of the back wall of the exhibition room. The wall itself was flat and smooth, painted a rather insipid eggshell colour.

Each alcove was the same shape: a precise, rectangular recess into the wall, about twenty-five centimetres wide and about forty centimetres high. Their back surfaces were curved, so that each formed a kind of deep, semi-circle scoop out of the wall.

In the alcove that was a few metres to the left of the empty Eye-of-the-Serpent-less one, there was a delicate-looking, white figurine of a lady with elongated arms and legs. In the alcove to the right was a vase, its shape composed of gliding curves. Beneath every alcove was a printed sign, decribing the piece and its place in art history. The one in front of me began:

The Eye of the Serpent
c.1929
*A rare example of the work of **Enid Bottomby**,*
almost the greatest artist of the 20th century . . .

The sign seemed rather lost and lonely, sitting there underneath an empty space, describing something that was long gone.

I walked up and down from one alcove to another, glancing at the lights suspended from above and the thin metal strip that ran along the floor a thumb's-width in front of the wall.

'You have to stand quite close to these alcoves to see what's in them, don't you?' I said. 'They're quite deep.'

'Yes, they were originally meant for putting trailing houseplants in.'

'In fact,' I said, pacing to and fro a couple of times, 'you have to look at them almost straight on. Are the lights always kept like this? One pointing at each alcove?'

'So I'm told,' said James. 'This end of the room gets

very little light from the window. You have to have the spotlights on all time.'

Peering into the empty alcove, I flipped the Whitehouse C-Anything Ultra-Vision Spex out of my top pocket and put them on.

James stared at me. 'Where did you get those hideous glasses? They look like something Muddy's mum would wear.'

'Shut up,' I muttered.

Through the specs I could suddenly see a spectacular network of red laser lines. They criss-crossed up from the metal strip in the floor, forming a tightly woven net across the entire wall.

'That's really cool,' I said, smiling.

'Those glasses aren't,' mumbled James.

I'd wondered if perhaps it was possible for someone to reach *through* the net of beams and take the statuette that way. But the only way it could have been possible would be for the thief to have fingers like pipe cleaners. And for the statuette to be equally narrow.

I was *so* tempted to reach out and break the beams! Just to see what would happen.

'I can see what you're thinking,' said James. 'Don't. I did it yesterday by accident, before the guests arrived. Those alarms are deafening.'

Keeping the C-Anything Ultra-Vision Spex on, I

turned around to look at the rest of the room. I could now see that every display had a net of laser beams around it!

'That's really cool too,' I said, grinning.

Then I suddenly stopped grinning. I took the specs off again. I made sure I was standing in front of the empty alcove, looking away from it. Something very odd was going on here.

'Are the display stands positioned like this for a reason?'

'I don't think so,' said James. 'They're all movable. They can go anywhere. You can put them in different places for different exhibitions.'

This was *very* odd.

'Where were you when the statuette vanished?'

James pointed. 'On that seat over there.'

'Go and sit down,' I said quietly. 'Show me exactly.'

He walked over to a black leather padded bench about ten metres away and sat at one end of it. I shut one eye, held out one arm like an arrow, and did a sweep from left to right, keeping my feet absolutely still.

'From here,' I called to James, 'I can see you, at the edge of that bench and I can see that door over there, with *Staff Only* on it —'

'That's the office,' said James.

'And that's all. Everywhere else, from this spot,

there's a display of some kind within a couple of metres.'

I tried to imagine myself in various parts of the room, facing in the direction of the spot on which I was now standing. A chilling possibility had popped into my head!

Remembering what James had just told me about those display stands, I now realised that one of the three questions I'd asked him yesterday – one of those three questions relating to the guests – was totally irrelevant. This statuette, The Eye of the Serpent, was a top exhibit here, and yet . . .

Have you worked out what was going through my mind?

'These displays,' I said carefully, 'can be placed anywhere, and yet they've been placed in such a way that the exhibition's most valuable piece can't be seen from most places in the room.'

'Yes, you're right,' said James, trotting back from the bench and looking away from the alcove as I'd just done. 'That's a bad bit of floor-planning. You've got to be right in front of it before you can see it.'

'Hmm,' I said quietly. 'I asked you yesterday if any of the guests had seen the statuette vanish. Now I can see that it would have been *impossible* to see the statuette vanish unless you were sitting right there, on that bench, or standing right there, by that office door. Or, of course, standing right here in front of it.'

'Yes,' said James. 'That really is bad floor-planning. Pity, when all the displays look so good.'

'You're missing my point,' I said, in a low voice. 'If all these displays can be placed anywhere, then there's the distinct possibility that they were deliberately placed to *hide* the statuette from most of the room. A perfect situation if you wanted to steal it with minimum risk of being seen.'

James frowned and shook his head. 'No, no, surely that would mean . . .'

If this possibility turned out to be correct, then there were clear deductions to be made. Deductions about the guests and about the person who committed the crime. I could even name my Suspect No 1!

Have you worked out what I was thinking?

If the displays had been positioned to deliberately *hide* the statuette, this would imply that the crime was committed by *someone on the staff of the gallery*. Why? Because they were the only ones who'd have access to the displays, and could have moved them. All the guests could therefore be taken off my list of suspects.

'But perhaps one of the guests quietly moved a couple of the displays?' said James. 'Perhaps they spotted that there was a way to conceal the theft from view?'

'Not with that brand new, high-power laser beam security net in place,' I said.

'Ah,' said James, 'but I thought you said that the alarm system must have been turned off, or disabled somehow? Otherwise the theft was impossible?'

I thought for a moment, my mouth twisting and wriggling into a series of 'hmmmm' and 'let's see now' poses. 'No, I don't think so,' I said. 'A guest couldn't start moving displays around, not without drawing a lot of attention to themselves! I'm sure you'd have noticed them, for a start.'

'True,' shrugged James.

'Which means that my Suspect No 1 has to be —'

'Davina,' said James. 'Because she designed the exhibition, and was therefore in the best position to place the displays in a way which would suit the thief.'

'Correct,' I said.

36

James shifted about uncomfortably. 'But I find it hard to believe it was Davina. She's so nice.'

'Nice doesn't mean innocent,' I said sadly. 'I've dealt with cases in which there were some highly unlikely culprits. Anyway, we can't say she *did* do it. We have no proof. There's plenty more investigating to be done. She's simply at the top of the list of suspects.'

Kla-klump!

The door to the office whumped shut and I turned to see a smartly-dressed man heading towards us. His face was deeply lined, with a bulbous nose and eyes which reminded me of a rodent. His hair was grey, cut into a short, spiky style, and he wore glasses with small, round lenses in a bright orange frame. He walked in a kind of skip-shuffle, which gave the impression he was permanently bursting for a wee. James explained that this was Morris Pettibone, the manager of the gallery.

'James, James, James,' called Mr Pettibone, 'Davina said you were here. Please get the seating set out as soon as possible, thank you, thank you.' His voice was low and drawling, as if it wanted to have a lie-down in a darkened room.

As he skipped up to us, he suddenly appeared to notice me for the first time. 'Who is this?'

'Hi, Mr Pettibone, this is my friend Saxby,' said James.

'He's a what?' said Mr Pettibone, blinking at me.

'My name's Saxby,' I said. 'Saxby Smart.'

His head twitched as if something in his brain had just given his memory a slap. 'Ah yes, James's father has told me about you, the boy who thinks he's a detective, am I right, am I right?'

'You couldn't be more right-er!' I said with a smile.

Mr Pettibone glared at me for a moment or two. 'Are you here to help out with the seating too?' he said.

'No, I'm here to help out with investigating last night's robbery,' I said. 'Could I ask you some questions?'

He glared at me a little more. 'No, you may not. Your help will not be needed – I'm only interested in the services of professionals, not under-aged amateur sleuths.' He said the word 'professionals' very slowly and deliberately, leaning forward slightly as he did so. 'This is a very grave matter, not the sort of thing that can be left in the hands of a schoolboy,' he said. 'It is an inquiry into a serious crime, not some playground game. Now unless you're willing to help out with the seating I'd like you to leave. We are very busy today, as I'm sure you can appreciate.'

'Tell you what,' I said, smiling sweetly at him. 'Why don't I forget about the detective work and help out with the seating instead?'

He eyed me like an eagle eyeing up some prey it thinks might explode and blow its beak off. But then, all of a sudden, his gaze seemed to soften. He shook his head, ran a hand across his stubbly chin and let out a long, shuddering sigh.

'Thank you very much, thank you,' he said. 'I do apologise if I seem short-tempered today, young man, my patience is stretched to its outer limit, the strain and anxiety of this awful business has deprived me both of sleep and of my manners, you'll forgive my rudeness – awful business, awful business.'

'Oh, so can I get on with the detective work after all?' I chirped.

'No,' he said. 'Help James with the seating. I mean it – leave the detective work to the police, or my temper will boil over, absolutely boil over.'

He turned and skip-shuffled away towards the entrance to the exhibition room, rapidly checking the displays to either side of him as he went. (It suddenly occurred to me that those glasses of his were even more hideous than the ones I'd borrowed from Muddy!)

'By the way,' I said, 'what's this seating for?'

'I told you this morning,' said James, 'Mr Pettibone is holding a press conference. He's got the police bloke in charge of the investigation coming, plus a load of reporters, plus people from the TV and radio.'

'And he's organised all this since the robbery last night?' I said.

'Yes,' said James. 'He had Davina phoning people this morning while I was visiting you in your shed.'

We left the exhibition room and headed through a maze of creaking hallways and dusty galleries, James leading the way. We collected a large wheelie-trolley of stacked-up plastic chairs from the small loading bay at the rear of the building, and heaved it all the way back to the Art Deco Experience, its left-side wheels turning in a slow, lopsided wobble.

By the time we got back, Mr Pettibone was pacing to and fro beside the glass door, picking nervously at his fingernails and checking his watch every few seconds.

'Ah, there you are boys, chairs in three semi-circular rows in front of the table please, chop-chop, no time to lose, where's Davina got to, where is that girl, where is she, where's Davina?'

Davina appeared from the direction of the office, her high-heeled shoes *clop-clicking* on the tiled floor like a startled pony. She held a bulging folder in one hand and balanced a tall mug of tea in the other.

'Did you immerse the teabag for no more than seven seconds?'

'Yes, Mr Pettibone,' said Davina, out of breath.

'No milk, one and one-fifth sugars?'

'Yes, Mr Pettibone.'

'Place the information hand-outs about the stolen

40

item where the reporters can find them easily, make sure there is clear access for the television crews —'

'Yes, Mr Pettibone.'

'And for goodness' sake do something about the Art Nouveau to Art Deco display, the heading is still one centimetre too low, please correct it, must I do everything myself around here?'

'Yes, Mr Pettibone. I mean, no, Mr Pettibone.'

'Well, come along all of you, get a move on, the press will be here any second, any second now.'

'Yes, Mr Pettibone,' we all said together.

James and I set out the chairs. Davina set the mug of tea down on the table she'd already placed in front of the huge *Welcome to the Art Deco Experience* sign that hung close to the entrance to the exhibition room. On the table was a crisp, clean white tablecloth, and behind the table were two chairs, one for Mr Pettibone, and one for:

'Inspector Godalming, welcome, welcome, do sit here,' said Mr Pettibone.

A short, uniformed police inspector had arrived. He nodded a greeting to Mr Pettibone and took his seat behind the table. Inspector Godalming had a face which seemed to be specially designed for scowling, and he moved in a quick, clipped way, like an oversized bird on the lookout for tasty worms.

'Let'sh hope thish presh conferensh resultsh in shome

41

promishing leads, Mr Pettibone,' he said. He clearly had a set of badly-fitting false teeth, too. I tried not to giggle.

'Indeed, Inspector, indeed,' sighed Mr Pettibone, dabbing a handkerchief to his forehead. 'I have had not one moment's rest since last night, not one moment, one single moment, my nerves are flayed, torn, broken, devastated.'

He took his seat next to the Inspector. By now small groups of media people were arriving too. Some of them had notebooks, some had microphones and some had cameras, but all of them looked eager to find out more about the robbery. They plonked themselves down on the plastic chairs we'd set out and chatted quietly to each other.

However, at that moment my attention was on Davina. She was standing to one side of the table watching Mr Pettibone sip his tea. The sour look on her face might simply have been indigestion. However, it seemed more likely that she was thinking: I hate you so much, Pettibone, that one day I'm going to poison your tea, chop you into little bits and then dance on your grave singing a merry tune, you pompous, weird-looking, hideous-spectacled twerp. Something like that.

It was time for me to investigate my Suspect No 1 a little more closely . . .

CHAPTER
FOUR

'LADIES AND GENTLEMEN, THANK YOU for coming here this afternoon,' announced Mr Pettibone. In front of him cameras watched, microphones listened, and notebooks got scribbled in. 'Last night a serious crime was committed in this very room, the theft of an extremely rare and valuable masterpiece entitled the Eye of the Serpent, one of the few surviving pieces by Enid Bottomby, almost the greatest artist of the twentieth century. I, Morris Pettibone, manager of this beautiful and important new gallery, have called you all here today for one simple reason, that reason being that we are launching a national campaign to find this stolen treasure and restore it to pride of place in our wonderful exhibition, the Art Deco Experience. I will now hand you over to Inspector Godalming, who will give you the horrific details of yesterday evening's events.'

Inspector Godalming cleared his throat noisily. 'H'I am the poleesh h'offisher leading thish h'inveshtigation . . .' he began. (I really must write his words without the whistling false teeth – I'm having trouble working out the spelling! Just take the whistling as read . . .)

James tapped me on the shoulder and indicated for us to retreat to the office. 'I think we'll have heard all this before,' he whispered.

I nodded and followed him. The office was a large, plain-looking room, with a narrow window on one side and a load of filing cabinets on the other.

However, what got my attention first of all was the wide, curving desk. It took up about a quarter of the space and it was bristling with the very latest in high-tech computer gear. None of it was switched on at the moment but it looked like the sort of set up that would glow around the edges when you booted it up, probably in a nice shade of blue. It looked like it would hum quietly and smugly to itself every time someone typed at its elegantly sculptured keyboard. This was the sort of computer gear that you just couldn't help but go 'Oooo' over.

'Oooo,' I said. 'I bet Muddy would love to get his mitts on this little lot.'

'Snazzy, isn't it?' said James. 'Nobody is allowed to touch it without Mr Pettibone's permission. In writing.'

'Why does an art gallery need stuff like this?' I asked, admiring the way that the whole thing was connected wirelessly, so that no leads or cables were left dangling about like a pot of spilled noodles.

'Davina uses it a lot,' said James. 'You see that long box-thing there, the one that looks a bit like a giant paper shredder? That's a high-resolution printer. All the signs and labels for the whole building are printed on it. The blown-up photos and display boards out there in the Art Deco exhibition were done on it, too. It'll print on anything from ordinary paper to huge sheets of thick, glossy card. This whole kit cost a fortune, but when you can do all those labels and displays right in the office it actually saves a lot of time and money in the long run. My dad's done some signs for our museum on this gear, actually.'

'Oooo,' I said.

As I looked around, I noticed another door, half blocked by one edge of the desk.

'Where does that go?' I asked.

'Oh, that's an old walk-in cupboard. I don't think it's ever used.'

Out of curiosity, I turned the doorknob and peered inside. It was completely empty, dark and windowless and so small that the door bumped against the opposite wall. The floor was evenly layered with a thick film of dust, and there was an odd smell in the air. A sort of clean, bathroomy smell I couldn't quite place.

'D'you want a drink?' asked James. 'I'm afraid they only have coffee, fizzy bottled water, or Mr Pettibone's herbal-tea-with-a-strange-name.'

'Thanks, I'll have a fizzy water,' I said, closing the door to the tiny storage room and having a bounce on one of the office's posh swivel chairs. 'Umm, I don't suppose they've got any chocolate biscuits?' I added innocently.

James hunted amongst the bottles and packets on top of the filing cabinets. 'No, but they've got some spongy cake things with jam in.'

'Oooo.'

James pointed out a keypad attached to the wall, with an LED screen above it blinking the word *Armed* in red letters. 'That's the alarm system. You turn it on and off with a four-digit combination. It's still set at its default: 1-2-3-4 – they've been too busy to change it.'

While we were sipping our fizzy water and gobbling down our spongy cake things with jam in, I noticed a small glass vase sitting at the back of the desk, beside the wall. I frowned slightly. What was that odd, rectangular background it was standing against? Was that some sort of frame around it?

I reached out to touch it. My fingers knocked against something hard and hollow-sounding. With a smile, I realised it was just a photo stuck on to a piece of light board, a bit like polystyrene.

'I told you,' said James, 'that printer does brilliantly high resolution —' He stopped and suddenly grinned. 'Hey, wait a minute, you thought that was a real vase, didn't you!'

'No!' I said, going a bit red.

'That's a cut-out left over from the exhibition,' said James.

'Yeah, I knew that,' I said hurriedly.

Luckily, I was saved from further embarrassment by the interruption of Davina, *k-klopping* into the office. She flashed us a sunny smile and thudded the box of leaflets she was carrying down on to the desk.

'Now then,' she gasped, 'where are those exhibition catalogues from last night? Mr Pettibone wants them available in case any of the reporters want to . . . Ah! There they are!'

She scooped up a pile of them, flashed us another sunny smile and *k-klopped* back to the press conference. As the office door opened and shut we could hear Inspector Godalming saying that the theft of the shtatuette wassh a total myshtery.

I picked up one of the catalogues. It was printed on to beautifully smooth card with pictures of all the exhibits shown next to detailed descriptions of them. It was also unusually large: there were only four pages to it, but these pages were the size of a small poster!

'Done on this whizzy printer?' I asked.

James nodded.

'But why is it so big?' I said. 'Surely last night's guests would have had trouble reading it *and* balancing their wine and celery nibbles at the same time?'

'Oh, you know these arty-farty types,' mumbled James, through a mouthful of spongy cake thing with jam in it. 'Doesn't matter if you can *use* it or not, it's got to *look* right.'

Davina bustled back into the office. For once she wasn't carrying an armful of anything. Instead, she was applying a fresh coating of lipstick, pulling faces into a little round make-up mirror.

'I've got a couple of minutes,' she gasped. 'Mr Pettibone's busy telling the reporters how shattered his nerves are.' She set about making herself a cup of coffee.

A-ha! Time for me to question my Suspect No 1!

'Do you mind if I ask you about last night?' I said.

'No, go ahead,' she said, fetching milk from the miniature fridge on top of the filing cabinets. 'Oooo, are those spongy cake things with jam in I see? Yummy.'

She perched on the chair beside the computer and hooked her hair back behind her ears. Her long fingers danced in mid-air, as if she was trying to remember something or running through a To Do list in her head.

'I see you're kept pretty busy here,' I said.

'I certainly am,' she said, still out of breath. 'Oh well, better than having nothing to do, eh?'

'True,' I nodded.

I wasn't sure whether I should ask my next question or not. If she *was* involved in the theft, this question might make her become suspicious of me. However, her reaction to it might tell me something, one way or the other.

So I went ahead and asked: 'Do you and Mr Pettibone get on OK? I couldn't help noticing that he can be a bit, umm . . . demanding?'

Her eyes stretched and she sipped her coffee. 'Demanding, yes, yes. Demanding. That would be a diplomatic way to put it, yes. Demanding. He is indeed.' She shook her head and waved a hand as if swatting unkind thoughts out of her way. 'Sorry, I don't mean to sound like I'm complaining. Really, he's a very nice man and very knowledgeable about art. He's extremely well connected in the art world, you see. He does lecture tours to universities. Half the art students in the country would love to have my job!'

'But, er, do *you* love your job?' I asked.

'I do,' said Davina, nodding. 'Really, I do. Mr Pettibone can be a so-and-so, yes. I mean, sometimes I feel like, y'know, poisoning his tea, chopping him up into little bits and dancing on his grave singing a happy tune. But only sometimes. I really am lucky to have got this job. I love being around all this wonderful art. Art Deco's a real favourite of mine, actually, I'd collect it myself if only I had the money.'

'Really?' I said, raising an eyebrow.

'Yes, it was such a shock when the Eye of the Serpent disappeared,' said Davina. 'That was one of my favourite pieces. And an Enid Bottomby as well!'

'Were you here when the police came last night?'

'Yes,' she said. 'They were really cheesed off that Mr Pettibone had let all the guests go home. They were tutting and "awww"-ing all over the place. They said the investigation might take months now, instead of days! They said it was even possible that the statuette would never be recovered. I think that's why they're keen on today's press conference, and Mr Pettibone's idea of a national appeal to find it.'

I didn't say anything about my earlier deductions (the ones which indicated that a guest was unlikely to be the culprit, and that the theft was probably done by someone involved with the gallery). If I'd said anything, she'd have realised that she was on my list of suspects. Even so, a further couple of important questions occurred to me . . .

'How many people work in this gallery?' I said.

'Oh, about fifteen or twenty in all,' said Davina. 'But Mr Pettibone and I were the only ones here last night.'

'Nobody else? Not a security guard, someone like that?'

'It didn't seem necessary,' said Davina. 'Not with our state-of-the-art alarm system switched on.'

'Could another employee have sneaked in?' I said. 'Mingled with the guests, perhaps? Hidden somewhere, waiting to strike?'

'Hardly,' piped up James. 'I was under strict instructions to only let people into that exhibition room if they had an invitation. With their name on it.'

'What about through this office window?' I said.

'It's jammed shut,' said Davina. 'We've got to get someone in to fix it. Honestly, I know everyone who works here and Mr Pettibone *hired* everyone who works here. We'd have noticed anyone like that straightaway.'

I thought for a moment or two. It seemed that every line of questions was leading into a dead end! There had to be something I wasn't seeing here, or something that I wasn't looking at in the right way.

'I assume the police searched this building,' I said.

'Oh yes,' said Davina, 'top to bottom, inside and out.

Every room, every drawer in every desk. They were in here for half an hour going through the filing cabinets. They were going to get flashlights and look in that walk-in cupboard over there, but they opened the door and could see that nobody had been in there for ages.'

'Yes, of course,' I muttered to myself.

'*How* did they know?' asked James. 'Have they got some sort of looking-back-through-time scanner or something?'

It was a clear-cut deduction. Think back to what I saw when I opened that door. Have you spotted what James hadn't?

'There's an undisturbed layer of dust on that floor,' I said. 'If anyone had so much as put a foot in there, it would show. In fact, it would look suspicious if there *wasn't* a layer of dust in there. That would imply that someone had been in there and cleaned the floor to eliminate their footprints!'

'Whoever took the Eye of the Serpent took it with them out of the building,' said Davina. 'I've got a horrible feeling that the police are right, and that it might never be found.'

I took my notebook out of my pocket and flipped through to the next blank page. 'OK,' I said, decisively. 'I need details. James, you've told me what you were doing when the statuette vanished. Davina, I need you to give me an *exact* break-down of what you did and where you were, starting at a point in time a short while before the theft.'

Davina took a deep breath and scrunched up her eyes in thought. Her lipsticked lips squashed into a concentrated 'O'.

Here is what I wrote down, based on what Davina then told me (plus a few interruptions here and there from James). Pay close attention to this, it'll become vitally important for the solving of the crime:

THE ROBBERY – from Davina's angle

Time: 7:15 p.m. Mr Pettibone tours exhibition to make sure everything's perfect; Davina told by Mr Pettibone to adjust the *Welcome* sign by two centimetres; once done, Davina goes to office and switches alarm system ON. (Comment from James: 'Yes, I saw her do that! I was in the office trying one of the celery nibbles and then spitting it out into the waste-paper basket.')

Time: 7:25 p.m. Davina chats to James about Enid Bottomby; James boggle-eyed – keeps wary eye on Serpent from this point on.

Time: 7:30 p.m. Guests now arriving; James collecting up invites at the door; Davina applies lippy, then stands around handing out those huge catalogues. (Mr Pettibone does the same.)

Time: roughly 7:45 p.m. All guests have now arrived – room very busy; Davina tours room with wine; James tours room with celery nibbles; Mr Pettibone still handing out catalogues, now chatting with Mayor about art history; Mayor pulling faces, clearly bored to tears (*or* possible allergic reaction to celery nibbles).

Question from me: Was the office door locked, or secured in any way?

Answer: No.

(Comment from James: 'But it did have *Staff Only* on it!'

Comment from me: 'Yes, James, that would be sure to stop any hardened criminal dead in their tracks!' Comment from James: [unrepeatable].)

Time: can't be exact, but within next few minutes. Mr Pettibone snaffles Davina's last glass of wine; Davina returns to office to fetch more; when she gets back, James tells her he's fed up of people saying, 'Don't you look grown-up in your suit and bow tie, young man!'

Time: 8:00 p.m. Davina sees James go to office, to refill tray of nibbles. (Comment from James: 'I was as quick as possible. I didn't want the Eye of the Serpent doing something curse-related without me seeing it!')

Time: 'Must have been roughly 8:05 p.m.' Davina sees old friend amongst guests – has brief conversation; Mr Pettibone notices guests have been leaving empty wine-glasses on windowsill – tells Davina to collect them up; Mr Pettibone goes to office to make short phone call; James flops on to bench.

Crime coming up NOW!

Time: 8:07 p.m. (exactly – Davina looks at wristwatch). Mr Pettibone (back from phone call) returns to lecturing Mayor on art history, shows him the Serpent – Mayor's face-pulling now at worrying level, ambulance may be needed; James watching statuette intently from bench; Davina flagged down by Mr Pettibone – he puts his now-empty wine glass on her tray, tells her to fetch more wine for guests from office; she heads for office door, but as she reaches it, she slips on someone's spilled wine – goes *woooaaahh* flat on her back with a squeal, tray of glasses crashes everywhere; Davina very relieved that Mr Pettibone had agreed to plastic glasses, otherwise could have been a serious accident; as it is, Davina highly embarrassed, plus has nasty smack on bum – notices that not only has the entire room looked in her direction, but James is smirking uncontrollably.

(Comment from James: 'Sorry, Davina, but it *was* very funny.'

Comment from Davina: [unrepeatable].)

Time: a couple of seconds later. Mr Pettibone rushes to help Davina; Davina attempts to dry wine-soaked trousers with paper napkin; guests carry on guzzling wine and nibbles; James carries on smirking.

Time: a couple of seconds later, again. Davina not happy – wine has soaked through to knickers; Mr Pettibone quickly tidying up glasses and soaking up rest of spilled wine with more paper napkins; sudden cry of 'Look, everyone! The Bottomby's gone!'; Davina turns to see James, standing, pointing at the now-empty alcove.

Exact sequence of events, from 8:08 p.m.:

• Guests freeze for a second, not sure what's happening.

• Mr Pettibone gawps at empty alcove, cries out in horror; then cries out, 'Nobody move! The Bottomby! Oh my God!'

56

- Guests crane necks and shuffle about to get a look at the empty alcove.
- Mr Pettibone cries out again, 'Clear the room! Call the police!'
- General confusion – Mr Pettibone tells Davina to get people back from the scene of the crime; Davina, with soggy trousers, hobbles in her high-heels across room, shoo-ing guests towards entrance.
- James is standing there, jaw as slack as a wet paper bag.
- Guests are grouped by entrance – all wondering what's happened, talking in low whispers; Mr Pettibone hurries over to empty alcove, stands there staring in horror, mumbling, 'It's gone! The Bottomby! Gone!'
- Davina goes over to Mr Pettibone; Mr Pettibone rooted to the spot, tells Davina to get the guests out of here then call the police immediately.
- Davina and James herd guests back through gallery to main entrance; Davina calls out calming announcements apologising for cutting the event short and assuring everyone that whatever it is that's happened, everything will be back to normal soon.
- At main entrance, James phones his dad to come and pick him up.
- Davina returns to exhibition; Mr Pettibone still rooted to spot, still mumbling in horror.
- Davina calls police from office.

Question from me: Was the alarm system still on?

Answer: Yes. I'm positive. I deliberately looked to see it was working, and it was.

Time: 8:35 p.m. Police arrive; Inspector Godalming says rude words when told all the guests have gone; Mr Pettibone's lower lip wobbles.

Time: 8:40 p.m. Davina switches off alarm system so police can investigate alcove – they dust for fingerprints; none found.

End of Davina's account.

Follow-up note from James: 'I overheard my dad calling Mr Pettibone later on. He told him to get Saxby Smart on the case! Dunno what Mr Pettibone said.'

I flipped back and forth through my scribbled notes.

James could back up Davina's account, right up to the point when he went home. So, if these notes provided me with an accurate run-down, then I could now say who'd had the chance to switch the alarm system off during the robbery!

Look back through Davina's account. Can you spot who had an opportunity to disable the laser net?

If I now had a reliable account of events, then Mr Pettibone or Davina or James could have done it. All three of them were alone in the office at some point between the start of the evening and the robbery. Normally, I wouldn't have expected James to know how to turn the system on and off as the other two would, but he'd told me that he also knew the four-digit combination (look back to page 46!).

This still left Davina as Suspect No 1 as she was still the most likely person to have carefully positioned those displays (to help conceal the crime, remember). Plus, I found it very hard to believe that *James* stole the statuette. For loads of reasons.

Mind you, stranger things have happened . . . *Could* he be involved? *Could* he have got *me* involved as part of some strange double-cross?

It was all very frustrating. I still had no *proof*. And I still had no idea whatsoever about *how* the statuette had been taken, alarm system or no alarm system! *Nobody* had been close enough to the Eye of the Serpent to take it during those crucial few seconds. Or rather, none of my suspects had been close enough: James was by that bench, and Mr Pettibone and Davina were over by the office door, mopping up wine.

I was sure that the solution was right in front of me. I was sure that all the pieces of the puzzle were here for me to see. I simply couldn't work out how they all fitted together!

'I've got to get back to the press conference,' said Davina, hopping to her feet. 'It's poor Mr Dubrovnik I feel really sorry for.'

'Who?' I said.

'Vladimir Dubrovnik,' said Davina. 'He's the collector we borrowed the Eye of the Serpent from. I had to call him this morning and give him the bad news. He was so angry I thought the phone would melt! That man's dedicated his life to the study and collection of Enid Bottomby's art. He's spent decades following every clue, researching every possible lead, in his quest to gather together the surviving examples of Bottomby's work.'

'That's amazing,' I said. 'How many has he got?'

'Two,' said Davina. 'They're *very* hard to find.'

'No wonder he's cross,' I muttered.

Davina headed back into the exhibition room. James and I followed, pausing only to scoop up the last of the spongy cake things with jam in.

The press conference was drawing to a close. Inspector Godalming was sitting with a carefully judged look of concern on his face and Mr Pettibone was facing the cameras, making a heartfelt plea for the statuette's safe return. Some of the reporters were beginning to compare notes and tap at their PDAs.

'And now,' said Mr Pettibone, 'if you'd like to follow me, there will be an opportunity to take pictures of the crime scene, thank you, this way, this way.'

I watched as photo flashes clustered and zapped around the empty alcove, with Mr Pettibone standing on one side of it and Inspector Godalming on the other.

Once again, I had a distinct feeling that the solution to this peculiar mystery was staring me in the face. What was it I was missing? What factor had I not taken into account?

Hearing about this Vladimir Dubrovnik character had reminded me that I needed to get some background info on this case. There was only one thing to do.

I called Izzy.

A Page From My Notebook

Question: Why is Mr Pettibone so against having my help? James's dad must have told him I cleared up the incident at the museum with my usual efficiency. You'd think Mr Pettibone would be grateful for any help he could get.

Question: I've been assuming that the view you could get of the Eye of the Serpent from the rest of the room was deliberately limited - but WAS it? COULD that simply be coincidence? Am I misinterpreting a simple oddity of floor layout?

Problem: Davina is still Suspect No 1 BUT she has an alibi (she was drying her trousers!). In fact, ALL my current suspects have an alibi (none of them were near the statuette when it vanished). AM I LOOKING IN TOTALLY THE WRONG DIRECTION? Have I made a mistake in thinking that none of the guests stole the statuette?

Problem: There's a strange mis-match here - the fact that the statuette is no longer in the building means, logically, that it was taken away, which implies, logically, that a GUEST is the thief. BUT! The fact that the alarm system was disabled implies, logically, that an INSIDER is the thief . . . So . . .

WAIT! WAIT! WAIT! Is THIS the missing bit? Could an insider have been working WITH one of the guests? The insider disables the alarms, the guest nicks the statuette? MUST THINK ABOUT THIS SOME MORE. ARGHHH!! This is driving me nuts! I have SEEN whatever there is to see and I have HEARD whatever there is to hear. But the answers seem as far away as ever. There is a connection I'm not making. There MUST be . . . mustn't there?

CHAPTER FIVE

THE NEXT MORNING, I WENT over to Izzy's house. On the way, I stopped to buy the local newspaper and a couple of the nationals as well. I wanted to see what they had to say about this case.

All of them had articles about the robbery. None of them really said much that was new to me but there were an interesting couple of paragraphs in *The Sunday Trumpet*, under the heading *Art Treasure Mystery – Police Foxed By 'Impossible' Theft From Gallery*. It said:

. . . The team of officers assigned to the investigation is being led by Detective Inspector Lionel Godalming, 55. He remarked, 'We are sure that a theft of this nature was the work of a large organised criminal organisation. It was without doubt carried out through the use of secretly drugged celery nibbles, by which the guests were rendered temporarily asleep.'

The owner of the stolen item, Vladimir Dubrovnik,
61, made a statement to local reporters in his home town
of Minsk, Russia. He said, 'This outrage destroys the
very fabric of civilised society. Those responsible should
be boiled alive in a vat of grease. If the Eye is not
recovered soon, I will consider offering a huge reward to
anyone – anyone at all – who can return it safely. And
I'm rich, so when I say huge, I mean huge. You know, not
just a few pounds. Huge.'. . .

I didn't realise it yet but the reward mentioned in this
article was an important link in the chain of clues that
would lead me to solving the riddle.

The trouble with most newspapers is they fall apart so
easily. By the time I arrived at Izzy's, there were folded-
up sections under each arm, the articles about the
robbery were stuffed into my pockets, and most of the
rest was gathered up in my arms in a crumpled heap. I
was pretty sure I'd also lost two or three sheets
somewhere between SuperSave and the Post Office.

Izzy stared at me for a moment when she saw me.

'Have you been trying to fold paper hats again?' she
said blankly.

'Oh, ha ha,' I said.

Isobel 'Izzy' Moustique is the St Egbert's School
in-house superbrain, the person I turn to whenever there

is in-depth research to be done. I'd phoned her the night before and given her the full story so far.

Up in her extraordinarily girlie room, she bounced on to the fluffy chair at her desk and started clattering away at her computer. Her fingers, which were overflowing with rings as usual, skipped rapidly across the keyboard and a series of files flipped open.

'Do you like the glittery edge I've put round my screen?' she said.

'Er, yes,' I said, not liking it at all. 'Very . . . attractive.'

As I was looking for something to sit on that wasn't a beanbag, I suddenly noticed movement on the other side of the room. Carefully, I leaned towards Izzy and whispered, 'There's a baby in here.'

Izzy swung around on her chair, grinning. The baby was blinking up at us from one of those kiddie car seats with a handle, happily dribbling away to itself.

'This is my latest cousin, Ben. We're looking after him for the weekend.'

'*Another* cousin?' I said, thinking back to the case *Whispers From the Dead*. 'How many have you *got*?'

She looked at me as if I was asking a really weird question. 'Only nineteen. Why? Ben's a wickle ickly sweetie pie, aren't you, eh, pookie pooooo?' She giggled at him, tapping his tummy to make him smile.

I felt slightly ill. 'Can we get on?' I asked.

Izzy squiggled the mouse beside her computer and the first of her files filled the screen.

'Given what you've already told me about this case,' she said, 'I've done some digging around this Eye of the Serpent, and around the gallery itself. But there's surprisingly little info available.'

'I was afraid of that,' I muttered. 'This case is knottier than a school tie in a knitting machine.'

She smiled at me, doing that arched eyebrow thing she does. 'Hmm. Could you have finally come across an insoluble mystery? Has Saxby Smart met his match?'

'Not in a million years,' I smiled back at her. I tried doing the eyebrow thing too but it was no good. Nobody can arch an eyebrow like Isobel Moustique.

'As for Enid Bottomby,' she said, 'it's true that she was a strangely unlucky person. She once broke both legs getting out of a car. All her hair turned green after a mix-up at the dentist's. She was struck by lightning, twice, on her birthday. I could go on for hours! Obviously, all that stuff about curses and so on is rubbish —'

'Obviously.'

'— but you can see where the stories come from. Half her life's work was destroyed by the last bomb to drop on England during World War II. She painted a famous portrait called *Daisy Reclining in the Afternoon*, which for years was thought to be lost, but then it turned up in a junk shop. It's only these stories surrounding her which have made her remaining work so valuable. Collectors go potty over her. Someone once paid two hundred thousand pounds for the overcoat button which got stuck in her windpipe in 1927. Nearly killed her.'

'So something like the Eye of the Serpent would be very hard for a thief to sell,' I mused. 'Without being found out, I mean.'

'Exactly,' said Izzy. 'Because it's a Bottomby, and therefore very, very famous in the art world. Frankly, stealing that Bottomby strikes me as completely pointless. There must be plenty of other pieces in that exhibition which a thief *could* sell undetected. Less valuable pieces, sure, but much more practical to nick!'

'Hmm,' I said. 'What about the gallery?'

'All I've got are a few facts and figures about Morris Pettibone,' said Izzy, clicking on to a new file. 'He comes from a very wealthy family, and owns houses in six different countries. He's written books on the history of painting and he even did a TV series on historic pottery about thirty years ago. What Davina told you was right: he's a real bigwig in arty circles. Or at least, he *was*. In the last few years he's been in charge of a whole series of disastrous projects. Do you remember a row about a sculpture in London a couple of years ago?'

'Er, yeah, was that the thing where it cost millions to put up, but everyone thought it was awful and it had to be taken away again?'

'That's the one,' said Izzy. 'And guess who was in charge? Morris Pettibone. Things like that have badly damaged his career. This new gallery cost a lot to set up, and he's under enormous pressure to make it a success. It's his last chance.'

'So a major robbery on opening night is absolutely the last thing he needed,' I said.

'Right,' agreed Izzy. 'It's no wonder it's doing his head in.'

'Glag glag gug ga,' said the baby. Or something similar.

'Is he hungweee?' piped Izzy, crouching down in front of the creature's throne. 'Don't you worry, ickle man, Izzy go get her mum, 'cos her mum got your wuvvery foodie-woodie, mmmmmmm!'

'Yes, well, if there's nothing else, I'll be off,' I said.

Izzy hoisted the baby out of his chair, and cuddled him delicately in her arms. 'He's so cute! Isn't he a ickle cutie-wootie-puddin'-pie, huh? Do you want to hold him?'

'No.'

'G'won,' said Izzy in the dopiest voice I've ever heard. 'G'won, he likes you, look, he's smiling. G'won.'

Suddenly, I smelled something.

I leaned forward, putting my nose close to the baby. I sniffed. Then I sniffed again, just to make sure I was sniffing what I thought I was sniffing.

'Oh dear,' said Izzy, 'has he done a giant poo again?'

'No,' I said. 'Nononono. Smell him. What does he smell of?'

Alarm bells were clanging in my brain. I'd come across this same smell before, very recently in fact. A sort of clean, bathroomy smell I couldn't quite place. Where had I encountered it? *Where?*

'Can't smell anything,' said Izzy. 'Unless you mean his talc?'

'His what?'

'Talcum powder,' said Izzy. 'You know, baby powder.'

'Actually, no, I don't,' I said.

'He's had a spot of nappy rash this week, haven't you, pookie-woo? You keep his bottom dry with a little bit of this white powder stuff, comes in a plastic shaker. I'm sure talc is rather old-fashioned these days, and Mum says that —'

I slapped my forehead. 'Of course,' I breathed. 'That's it. That's *it*! I've solved the case!'

Izzy pulled a face at me. 'What? Because of the smell of Ben's baby powder?'

'Absolutely!' I cried. 'I really *was* looking at things the wrong way around! *Now* I can see the connection I was missing! What a clever ickle baby-waby you are!'

Quickly, I thanked Izzy, zipped down the stairs, zipped down the road, and zipped off home. As I zipped, the elements of the crime gradually slotted together in my mind.

The thief had carried out a daring and risky plan. And I might never have pieced it all together, if I hadn't got a whiff of that baby!

The whole case revolved around a number of apparently unrelated things, including:

1. The exhibition catalogues which had been given out that evening.

2. That highly polished floor in the exhibition room.

3. The new late-night opening at James's dad's museum.

How much of the truth can you work out?

CHAPTER
SIX

THE FOLLOWING DAY, AFTER SCHOOL, I hurried over to the gallery. I'd been avoiding James all day because I knew he'd start nagging me to tell him what I'd discovered. I made sure I was first out of the school gates and then ran like the wind so he wouldn't catch up with me on the way.

He caught me before I got to the end of the street.

'You're *so* unfit!' he said.

I grumbled wheezily. I didn't actually say anything because I was too out of breath to speak. One of these days I really *must* start getting more exercise.

'What have you discovered? Awww, go on, tell me!' he said. He said it seventeen more times before we got to the gallery. By then I was ready to thump him.

'Let's just get inside, shall we?' I muttered crossly. 'Did

you make those phone calls I asked you to?'

'Yeah, yeah,' he said. 'What have you discovered? Awww, go on, tell me!'

Eighteen. Grrrrr.

Inside, the gallery was almost filled with visitors. The room that housed the Art Deco Experience was the busiest of all.

'Wow,' said James. 'I never expected to see so many people in here.'

'I did,' I said quietly.

The area around the crime scene had been cordoned off with blue-and-white tape which said *Police – Do Not Cross.* Assembled in this area were Davina, Mr Pettibone and Inspector Godalming.

'Hi everyone,' I said, with a wave. I was trying to look confident and businesslike, but I felt as nervous as a lamb chop in a tiger's cage. If I was wrong, I could end up in big trouble over this.

'I told you before,' said Mr Pettibone, with a face like granite, 'I am not interested in the opinions of amateurs, I am only here because my assistant Davina asked me to hear you out, is that clear, is it clear?'

'That's clear,' I said. 'I do appreciate your being here. And you, Inspector, I'm sure you're a busy guy.'

'I certainly am, sonny,' said Inspector Godalming. He snapped and shifted inside his uniform as if his arms and legs would much rather have been somewhere else. 'The investigation into this crime is going flat-out back at the station. I'm only prepared to hear your fanciful theories 'cos my chief constable says we got to listen to the community more. If you're wasting my time, sonny, well, that's, er . . . that's wasting police time. Very serious offence!'

'What is it you've got to tell us, Saxby?' said Davina. 'As you can see, the gallery's very busy today and I've got a lot to do.'

'Yeah, go on, tell us,' said James.

I took a deep breath. 'OK,' I began. 'If I'm correct, then in a matter of minutes I'll be able to place the Eye of the Serpent back in its proper place, in that empty alcove there.'

The four of them gawped at me. Then they turned and gawped at the alcove. Then they gawped at me again. In front of the *Do Not Cross* barrier, visitors shuffled along, examining exhibits and trying to overhear what was going on.

'The theft of that statuette,' I said, 'was a carefully calculated scheme. One which involved a great deal of personal risk on the part of the thief, but one which, if successful, would bring major rewards.'

'Quite right, sonny,' said the Inspector. 'That Bottomby's worth two million smackers! Sizable loot for a desperate gang of low-lifes!'

'I'm not talking about money, Inspector,' I said. 'That was the first mistake I made, assuming that this crime was carried out for money. That wasn't it. That wasn't it at all.'

'Then what was it?' said Davina.

'This crime had a totally different motive,' I said. 'I'll get to that in a minute.'

'If it wasn't done for money,' cried James, 'why would anyone steal it?'

'Well, y'know,' I said, 'in a funny way, the statuette was never quite *stolen*, as such. More sort of . . . moved.'

'The boy's talking nonsense,' grumbled Mr Pettibone. 'If you won't get to the point, child, kindly go away.'

'One thing made the disappearance of the statuette possible,' I said. 'The high-tech computer equipment over there in the office. It can take photos of things and turn them into high-resolution, beautifully printed displays. Displays which are good enough to, at least briefly, fool a casual observer into thinking they're looking at a real object. I was fooled for a moment into thinking I was sitting next to a real vase.'

'Hang on,' said Davina, 'are you saying that the Eye of the Serpent wasn't really there? That it was replaced with a lifelike photo?'

'No,' I said. 'I'm saying the exact opposite. I'm saying that a picture was taken of that *alcove* where the statuette

74

was to be placed. A picture of the *empty* alcove. Using the equipment in the office, you could print out that picture at life-size, cut it to be an exact fit in the real alcove, mount it on a board and place it in the alcove itself. Result? You'd look at the alcove and your eye would be fooled into thinking you were looking at an empty space. Not for long, and not if you examined it close up. But long enough. Long enough for someone a few metres away – that's you, James – to stand up and say, "Hey, guys, there's suddenly an empty space over there".'

'I get it,' said James. 'The alcove is a recess into the wall. So if you had a really top-notch photo of it, printed to the same dimensions as the alcove itself, and put them side-by-side, you wouldn't be able to tell them apart! Well, not straightaway.'

'Correct,' I said. 'This end of the exhibition room gets very little natural light. The spotlights have to be on all the time. In other words, the lighting at this end of the room hardly changes at all. You could easily make an actual-sized photo of the empty alcove look identical to the real alcove. Fit the photo into the alcove, and any object placed inside the alcove would be perfectly hidden.'

'But you'd have to look at the "covered-up" alcove straight-on,' said James. 'It wouldn't work the same if you looked at it from an angle.'

'Correct again,' I said. 'And that's precisely what you

have to do in this room. The view of that alcove is deliberately limited. You *do* have to look at it straight on, to get a good view of anything inside it.'

'Wow,' smiled James. 'That's *really* sneaky!'

Inspector Godalming shook his head, his shoulders squaring themselves up like soldiers on a parade ground. 'No no no, sonny,' he said. 'My men have examined that alcove every which way.'

'Inspector,' I sighed, 'I'm not saying there's a photo in the alcove *now*. It would only have been there for a matter of minutes, just until the thief had a chance to take the statuette away and leave the alcove empty for real. All the thief had to do was make the photo in the first place.'

Mr Pettibone turned slowly, his face sliding into an expression of absolute disgust. 'Davina, how could you, my trusted assistant, my loyal aide, my faithful —'

'W-what?' gasped Davina, wide-eyed. 'It wasn't *me*!'

'You're very skilled in the use of that computer,' said Mr Pettibone, dismayed. 'You created all these displays, you designed this entire exhibition, you did, you yourself.'

'Yes,' cried Davina, 'following *your* instructions!' Tears welled up in her eyes.

'Wait!' I said, loudly enough to cut them both off. 'Davina had nothing to do with it. She's completely innocent. Although, Davina, I have to admit you were Suspect No 1 right up until the last minute. Actually,

James, I wondered for a while if you'd been involved.'

'Eh? Thanks a heap!' grumbled James.

'But now I'm sure I was wrong,' I said.

This was the point of no return. I was now going to have to cross the line which would mean either success or failure.

'I think it was you, Mr Pettibone,' I said. 'You also had full access to that computer equipment.'

Mr Pettibone glared at me. 'So did a number of people, both gallery staff and others – even James's father has used that computer, as well you know.'

'Yes,' I said, carefully, a stab of nerves slicing through my stomach, 'but nobody else had your motive, and nobody else had the opportunity to remove the statuette from the alcove.'

'Watch what you're saying, sonny,' growled the Inspector. 'This is Morris Pettibone you're talking to, not some petty crook in a hoodie! He's a respectable citizen!'

'Are you claiming,' said Mr Pettibone, in a voice as icy as a frozen lake, 'that I walked up to this alcove, that I placed a mounted photograph in it, without anyone paying me the slightest attention, are you, are you?'

'Yeah, that's a good point,' said James. 'You'd still have to position the photo in the alcove. Surely you'd be seen?'

'This is where we have to remember the exact sequence of events on Friday night,' I said. I took my notebook from my pocket, and checked through my scribbles (refer back to pages 54-58 during this next bit, if you like).

'Just before eight o'clock,' I said, 'Mr Pettibone took a glass of wine from Davina's tray. So, he now has a full glass of wine in one hand and a pile of exhibition catalogues in the other. Everything is ready for him to put his plan into operation, he's just waiting for a convenient chance to begin.

'He spots his chance just a few minutes later. He goes to the office, apparently to make a phone call. But he doesn't make a phone call. He switches off the alarm system. Nobody can *see* that he's switched off the alarm system because those laser beams are invisible.

'He then comes back out. And here's a crucial bit: he deliberately spills that full glass of wine on to the floor, right outside the office door. He probably glances around to make sure nobody's looking in his direction. But even if someone *does* see him do it, oh dear, silly me, just an accident. Nothing suspicious.

'At this point, timing becomes important. People are milling about, there's a puddle of wine by the office door, he's got to act quickly. He collars Davina. He's already had her collecting up empty glasses. He now puts *his* empty glass on to her tray and tells her to return to the office to fetch more wine for the guests.

'She does as she's told. Now, I'm sure we've all noticed

two things: the floor in this room is highly polished, positively shiny; also, Davina's the sort of person who wears a lot of high-heeled shoes and tends to rush about the place. She hurries over to the office, straight into a puddle of liquid on a shiny floor. An accident waiting to happen? Absolutely.

'Bang. Down goes Davina. Almighty great crash of tray and glasses. What happens next?'

'Well,' said James, 'everyone turns to see what's happened.'

'Right,' I said. 'Any room full of people would do the same. You turn to look, James, and so do all the other guests. Only for a couple of seconds! But that's all the distraction that's needed. Mr Pettibone, and the Mayor, and one or two others, are a couple of metres away from the Eye of the Serpent. The mounted photo is popped on to the alcove the very second that the crash makes everyone turn to look.'

'But where did the photo come from?' said James. 'Did he have it stuffed down his trousers or something?'

'No,' I said, 'he had it hidden inside those exhibition catalogues. Those *big* catalogues. Those catalogues that were far larger than they needed to be. Everyone assumed that the size of the catalogues was just an arty-farty design thing on Mr Pettibone's part. But no, they had to be large enough to conceal a mounted photo inside.

'And then, just a few seconds after the crash, Mr Pettibone is over by Davina, helping her up. He's well away from the alcove now. All he's got to do is wait for someone to spot the "missing" statuette. He knows it won't take long. He doesn't know who'll spot it, but it just happens to be James.

'There's confusion! What's happened? People are starting to see that, yes, good grief, that statuette has vanished. Now, Mr Pettibone goes into his panic act. Clear the room, clear the room! He's GOT to get everyone out of there, before someone looks too closely. He's running lots of risks this evening but this bit is one of the riskiest. If the photo is spotted, it's all over. The Eye of the Serpent is tucked away behind it, hidden from view. Mr Pettibone gets Davina and James to usher the guests out.

'Leaving him, and only him, in the exhibition room. As Davina and James and the guests all leave he's still doing his I'm-so-stunned-I-can-hardly-stand routine. The moment they're all gone, he whips away the photo and takes the statuette. Then he goes to the office and switches the alarm system *back on*. By the time Davina returns, and goes to the office herself to call the police, Mr Pettibone is back in position in front of the empty alcove – which is now empty *for real* – doing his O-woe-is-me thing.

'Mr Pettibone wasn't the only one who had a chance to switch off the alarms that night. But he *was* the only one who had a chance to take the statuette. He was the only one who was left alone in that room.'

'Hang on a minute, sonny,' said Inspector Godalming. 'Why not, when the crash happens, simply take the statuette from the alcove and pop it into the bag of an accomplice? So then this other person can remove it from the premises and get it safely out of the building when the room is cleared?'

'Yes, I wondered about that too,' I said. 'But involving someone else in this scheme would be even *more* risky. Mr Pettibone was already running a lot of risks as it was, lots of things could have gone wrong. The last thing he wanted to do was risk being blackmailed, or double-crossed by a partner in crime, on top of everything else. He didn't *need* an accomplice. He could take the statuette and hide it all by himself. Why complicate matters?'

'This is the most preposterous rubbish I've ever heard,' snarled Mr Pettibone.

'My men searched this place top to toe,' said Inspector Godalming. 'Where could the statuette possibly have been hidden?'

'That's right,' said Davina. 'The police combed every inch of this building.'

'Not *every* inch,' I said. 'Can we go into the office now?'

'That does it,' growled Mr Pettibone, 'I've heard enough of this drivel, I'm a busy man, I'm going to —'

'No, let's see where the lad's going with this,' said the Inspector, gently taking Mr Pettibone by the arm.

We crowded into the office. Once everyone was settled, I stepped across the room and opened the door to the walk-in cupboard beside the desk.

'Take a look in here, Inspector,' I said. 'What do you see on the floor?'

'Dust,' said the Inspector. 'Nobody's been in there for a while, obviously.'

'That's what your men thought, too,' I said. 'That's what I thought. But that's not dust. That's a delicate sprinkling of talcum powder. Take a sniff inside. Notice the smell? That floor is another trick to fool the eye!'

'But the statuette isn't in there,' said Davina. 'You can see it's not.'

'You can't fully open this door,' I reminded her. 'It bumps against the opposite wall. If you wanted to see *behind* the door you'd have to squeeze into the cupboard, then close the door to look. And you'd still need a flashlight or something.'

'So you could go in there,' said James, thinking carefully, 'hide stuff, then sprinkle talc behind you to make it look like the cupboard hadn't been entered for ages?'

'Yup,' I nodded. 'Mind you, it wouldn't work if someone looked too closely. The talc would smear, you'd see it wasn't dust after all. But, like the photo, it would fool someone *just enough* to hide the truth.'

'But why hide anything in there?' said Davina. 'Why not quietly remove the statuette from the building? If it's in the building, it might be found.'

'Because of Phase Two of the thief's plan,' I said.

'Which is . . .?' said James.

'Which is when the statuette gets found "by accident". And the thief is "discovered".' (I put plenty of stress on those inverted commas!)

'Are you saying Mr Pettibone was planning on being found out?' said James.

'No, no, absolutely not,' I said. 'Let me explain Phase Two. Now, Phase Two *might* have been put into effect that same night, Friday night, *if* the talcum powder trick hadn't worked and the police had searched inside the cupboard. But! What Mr Pettibone was hoping – and this is what actually happened – was that the talcum powder trick *would* work, leaving him free to begin Phase Two at a later date. Possibly a *much* later date.

'You see, Phase Two is all about . . . how would you put it? Er, finishing the story. Closing the circle, so to speak. The Eye of the Serpent is stolen: this is Phase One. The Eye of the Serpent is recovered, and the thief unmasked: this is Phase Two. Of course, Mr Pettibone wasn't suddenly going to say 'Ooh look, here it is, everyone, I've found it, panic over!' Oh no. I can't be *sure* who he was intending to frame for the robbery, but my guess is that he was going to make sure Davina took the blame.'

'What?' spluttered Davina. 'How?'

'After a while,' I said, 'all Mr Pettibone would have to do is take the statuette out of its safe hiding place and put it somewhere it could be "unexpectedly discovered" by someone: your handbag, Davina, maybe, if it was big enough, or a shopping bag, or even somewhere in your home. It wouldn't be hard for him to find an excuse to call at your house one day, would it? Again, I can't be *sure* what was intended, but the end result would be Davina's arrest for the crime.

'And she'd look pretty guilty. She had the opportunity to disable the alarm; she was clearly under Mr Pettibone's thumb and had a reason to dislike him; she made no secret of how much she'd love to collect these Art Deco pieces herself; she knew all about the statuette and what it was worth; she was —'

'But what about her alibi?' said James. 'She was slipping over on that wine!'

'And Mr Pettibone was helping her up when the theft was spotted,' I said. 'He *appears* to have an alibi, too. It would end up as being *his* word against *hers*. Who would the police believe? Would they believe Davina when the statuette had just been found amongst her things? I doubt it. Don't forget, there was likely to be a reward offered for the statuette's return. It could easily be argued that Davina, knowing the statuette's owner as she did, had stolen the statuette so she could later pretend to track it down and then claim a load of cash! Mr Pettibone wouldn't look suspicious on that score – he's got plenty of his own cash, he'd have no need of reward money. No, Davina could be made to look very guilty indeed!'

'Th-th-that's awful!' spluttered Davina. 'Why would anyone do something like that? Why?'

'These allegations are getting more serious every minute, sonny,' said Inspector Godalming. 'You still haven't explained the reason for the theft in the first place.'

'Quite right,' I said. 'The last link in this chain is the motive for the crime. Remember, I said it wasn't done for money? Well, here's what it *was* done for: fame. Publicity.

'A little while ago, I unravelled a crime over at the town's museum, where James's dad works. James mentioned to me on Saturday that, since those events had come to light, the number of visitors to the museum had increased enormously. In fact, they'd increased so much that the museum now has late-night opening on a Friday. Right, James?'

'That's right,' said James.

'That crime,' I said, 'a robbery, appeared in the local papers, as you might expect. But it wasn't exactly national news. Travel more than a few miles from here and few people will have heard about it. And yet it had a huge effect on that museum.

'So. Imagine what effect a really *big* news story would have. On, ooh, let's say, for example, a new art gallery that was just opening. And lo and behold, what happens? *Art Treasure Mystery – Police Foxed By Impossible Theft From Gallery!* An art treasure which has stories about curses attached to it, no less! An art treasure which is very famous, and which will cause an uproar if it's lost!

'It was in all the papers yesterday. It's been on the radio and TV news. It's been everywhere. And now look outside the office! This gallery is packed out. On a Monday afternoon. Only a day or two after the theft.

'Mr Pettibone has held a press conference. Help us find the stolen statuette! Launch a national search! It *was* your idea, wasn't it, Mr Pettibone?'

'Are you daring to suggest that —?' began Mr Pettibone.

'Let the lad finish,' cut in the Inspector.

'For some years now,' I said, 'Mr Pettibone has been struggling to make a success of things. Which is very unfortunate. Nobody could possibly blame him for wanting to make this new gallery a hit. I'm sure we can understand the dreadful pressure he felt he was under. After all, if this place had turned out to be a flop, he'd have been finished in the art world.

'So he needed to make certain that the gallery got publicity, a lot of it, and became famous. He came up with a plan: a daring, apparently impossible robbery, followed by a national search, followed by the unmasking of his evil, dastardly assistant as the thief. It would all keep this place in the papers for days. Maybe weeks. Maybe even months, if he could string it out that long.

'And afterwards, people would *flock* here! People would organise *coach trips* just to come and get a look at this infamous, notorious, cursed piece of art! The Eye of the Serpent! Now returned to its place in the gallery, safe and sound, ladies and gentlemen.'

'Poppycock, balderdash, rubbish,' snarled Mr Pettibone. 'You have no shred of evidence, not a shred.'

'I promised you all that I'd produce the Eye of the Serpent for you,' I said, a sudden shudder of nerves sliding icily down my spine. 'If I'm right, if what I've told you is the truth, then the statuette is sitting exactly where I said it would be. It's behind the door of that walk-in cupboard, undisturbed since talcum powder was sprinkled on the floor in there, to put us off the . . . er, scent. Inspector? Would you do the honours?'

Inspector Godalming shot a look at me which said a heck of a lot, beginning with, 'If you're wrong . . .' and ending with '. . . you'll be in big trouble, sonny.'

He opened the cupboard door and squashed his way

inside. The talc on the floor was kicked up into a sweet-smelling cloud. For several seconds, the policeman bumped around in the dark, then emerged red-faced.

I couldn't see if he was carrying anything or not.

I held my breath. Was it there?

He held out his hand. Clutched in it was a sinewy, curling black object. He handed it to me.

It was surprisingly heavy. It had a smooth base, up from which flowed a coiling, curving shape. At the top was a large, ugly head, its mouth gaping, a single red jewel shining at its side.

'Eurgh, creepy, isn't it?' I muttered.

'The Eye of the Serpent,' gasped Davina. For a moment I thought she was going to burst into tears. I hurriedly handed it over to her.

'Here. I think you know where this should go,' I said.

Mr Pettibone was standing still and his face had gone very pale. Inspector Godalming turned to him.

'Mr Pettibone, I'd like you to accompany me to the police station,' said the Inspector. 'I believe you may be able to help us with our inquiries.'

He led Mr Pettibone towards the office door. The gallery manager was silent and slumped as he removed his orange spectacles and folded them up into his top pocket.

The Inspector turned to me. 'Well done, lad. Er,

obviously my men were, umm, about to come to the same conclusion. All that stuff about international criminal gangs was, er, just a smoke-screen, a cover-up, a way of putting Pettibone off-guard, y'see.'

'I see,' I said, nodding wisely. 'A brilliant trick it was, too. I never suspected a thing.'

Inspector Godalming nodded cheerfully at me and led Mr Pettibone away.

The next thing I knew, Davina was hugging me! Eugh, geroff! Too late, she'd planted a big wet smacker of a kiss on my cheek. 'Saxby, you're a marvel!' she gasped. 'If it wasn't for you I could have ended up in prison!'

'All in a day's work,' I mumbled. 'I'll be off home now.'

James and I made our way through the visitor-choked gallery and back out on to the street.

'I suppose Mr Pettibone got the idea after my dad had told him all about how well the museum was doing,' said James.

'Could be,' I said. 'Ah! I see now why Mr Pettibone didn't want me around!'

'Oh yeah, I get it,' said James. 'Dad must have told him about you, too. So naturally he didn't want you poking your nose in!'

'It's ironic, really,' I said. 'Mr Pettibone will get his wish. There'll be massive publicity over this, but for all the wrong reasons. *Respected Expert is Art Thief*, that's what the papers will say. Or maybe *Police Foil Art Crime.'*

'But you should take the credit!' said James. 'You solved the crime!'

'Nooooo,' I declared. 'I've said it before and I'll say it again, I don't do this job for applause, I do it to see truth and justice prevail.'

'Oh yes, I can see that,' said James. 'Otherwise you'd obviously have waited to reveal your findings. Until that Vladimir Dubrovnik bloke went ahead and offered that huge reward for the statuette's return. Obviously.'

Oh bum.

'Obviously, yes,' I said, feeling a bit weak and feeble. 'The work is its own reward.'

'Wow,' said James. 'That's positively heroic.'

'Yes, it is, isn't it?' I agreed.

'By the way, did you know your cheek's covered in lipstick?'

I just about had it wiped away by the time I got home. It left a bright red stripe across my sleeve.

I hurried to my shed, eager to write up some notes on the case. I swung the door open to find my desk buried under a pile of gardening equipment and DIY stuff. I sighed. I'd forgotten about that.

Double bum.

Case closed.

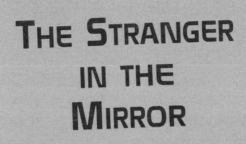

THE STRANGER
IN THE
MIRROR

CHAPTER ONE

I ONCE TACKLED A CASE IN which the most vital piece of
evidence was to be found by examining the cover of an old
hardback book, the *Colin the Hedgehog Annual 1997*: the
villain had written a note on a piece of paper and had used
the book to lean on. The pressing of the pen had gone
through and left a faint indentation on the book cover,
proving that the note was written in a particular place.

There was another case in which I would never have
identified the bad guy if he hadn't – totally by chance –
borrowed the same book from the school library as I had.
There was a page marked in the book which I wouldn't
have discovered without that one-in-a-million coincidence.

What I'm getting at is this: sometimes, crimes can be
solved (or even carried out) because of the tiniest little

details. *The Stranger in the Mirror* – a straightforward problem in many ways – was an interesting one because nobody could have predicted the series of events and coincidences around which the whole case revolved.

It began the day I came up with yet another idea in my battle to reorganise the garden shed. As you may have read in some of my other case files, I was determined to make more room for my detective kit in amongst the gardening and DIY stuff I'm forced to share that shed with. I was having about as much success as an ant trying to force a ten-ton weight up a waterfall backwards.

And then I thought: A-ha, why not simply push all the boxes and flowerpots and paint tins to the back of the shed? This will leave enough space for my desk, my files and my Thinking Chair, and possibly even that pacing-up-and-down area I wanted, too!

A couple of hours later, I'd finished. I was exhausted. I was also left with the same amount of floor space I'd have had in a small kitchen cupboard. My desk, notes and chair were all squashed up in a line. So much for *that* idea!

I was about to start yelling, jumping up and down, tearing my hair out and generally having a screaming fit, when there was a sharp knock at the shed door.

'Saxby? You in there?' called a commanding, posh-sounding voice. 'This is an emergency!'

Standing outside on the grass was Tom Bland, a

gangly, swirly-blond-haired guy from St Egbert's School. He was rarely in the same lessons as me, but I knew him well. Everyone at St Egbert's knew Tom Bland.

He was going to be the next Big Name in showbiz. So he said. To anyone who'd listen. He was in all the school plays, and he was convinced that he was, literally, the world's greatest actor. He *was* quite good, actually. But only quite good. The thing he was most famous for at St Egbert's was being a right drama queen. (Or should I say drama king? Drama-royal-person-of-some-kind, anyway).

'What's the emergency?' I said, poking my head out of the shed.

'This!' cried Tom, flapping a sheet of newspaper in my face. 'This! It's outrageous! It's a disgrace!'

Leaving the shed door open (otherwise we'd probably have run out of oxygen in there within a couple of minutes), I pointed him towards my Thinking Chair. With my stuff all squished in as it was, I had to wriggle on to the top of my filing cabinet. I had to hold on, too, to avoid sliding off.

'Start from the beginning,' I said. 'How can I help you?'

Tom took a deep breath or two, eyes closed.

'Take a look at this page from today's local newspaper,' he said, handing it over to me with a flourish. 'Steel your nerves, Saxby! Prepare to reel in horror!'

I opened out the page and read out the headline in

front of me. *'Dog Show Cancelled.'*

'Noooo,' he cried, 'the bit above that!'

I looked at the bit above that. There was a colour photo showing a kid of about our age, whom I didn't know. Standing behind him were two adults, presumably his parents, whom I didn't know. Standing next to them was a weird-looking man, with a T-shirt and a huge mouth, whom I also didn't know. The brief report beside the picture was headed: *Competition Winner Visits Radio Station.*

I wasn't reeling in anything very much, let alone horror.

'Look at the kid's name!' cried Tom.

I read the photo caption. *Pictured with his proud parents is Thomas Bland, whose winning entry earned him a VIP trip to the Vibe FM studios, and the chance to appear on the station's weekly Theatre Review show. 'The theatre is his dream,' said his mother Petula. 'He's very talented.'*

'So he's got the same name as you, and he also likes acting,' I said. 'Interesting coincidence. Incovenient if you ended up in the same school play, but hardly a crime.'

'No, no, you don't understand,' he wailed. 'That's supposed to *be* me! It was *me* who won that competition! Someone I don't know has stolen my identity! My name! And he's nicked my competition prize, too! It's an outrage! What am I going to do, Saxby? What am I going to dooo?'

See what I mean? A right drama queen/king/royal person.

CHAPTER TWO

'YOU'VE GOT NO IDEA WHO this kid is?' I asked.

'None!' cried Tom. 'I've never seen him, or his shabby-looking parents, in my life! How did he steal my prize? How did he even know I'd won it? Who *is* he? One thing I *do* know, he's a total *amateur*. I'd have made sure I got *twice* as big an article, *and* a bigger picture.'

'Hang on, hang on,' I said. 'What stopped you claiming this prize?'

Tom grimaced angrily. 'It's like this. I heard about the radio station's competition a few weeks ago. Although the prize didn't involve acting, as such, it was perfect for me because I'd be able to speak to the public about the theatre, the subject I know best. Also, of course, I'd get a chance to inform the listening millions about what a treat they'd be in for if they came along to one of my school play performances.'

I seriously doubted that a rubbish station like Vibe FM had an audience of millions. However, I let the point go. Tom was in full flow.

'So I prepared my entry, which had to be a review of a play I'd seen recently, and uploaded it to their website. The following week, one of the station's DJs – that's him there in the photo – phoned and said I'd won. Not a great surprise. My review was pretty good. He said the station would be sending me a package in the post, containing a load of Vibe FM freebies, and most importantly my Special VIP Golden Lucky Visitor's Pass. So far, so good. I waited, and waited, and waited. Nothing turned up. I was going to give it until tomorrow, and then ring this DJ and ask him to get his act together. But this morning, to my absolute *horror*, I see *this* in the local rag! It's appalling! Dreadful! Inexcusable! That wretched kid should be hurled into jail! The incredible *cheek* of it! I've never been so —'

'Yeah, OK,' I said, paddling both hands in mid-air to tell him to calm down. 'Let's examine this carefully. Have you spoken to the radio station today?'

'Of course,' cried Tom. 'I called them as soon as I saw *this* picture! They said the package was sent, and as far as they're concerned, I turned up, had a great time, and went home again! They suggested it was *me* who was the imposter! *Me!*'

'So I assume the imposter went ahead and appeared on this *Theatre Review* show? Did you hear it?'

'No. I had no idea *he'd* be on it! I said to that DJ this morning on the phone, wasn't he *aware* that this kid wasn't the one who'd written that superb winning entry? And you know what he said? He said, no he wasn't, but he *was* aware that the kid was a polite, well-mannered boy and not some rude, hysterical prima donna! Dreadful man!'

'Hmm, dreadful, yes,' I muttered. 'Did he say when the package was posted?'

'Yes, it went by first class, recorded delivery, the day after he originally called me. That meant it had to be signed for when it arrived. The postman would have to get a signature on his clipboard before handing the package over.'

'And that didn't happen?' I said.

'No,' said Tom. 'By my estimate, the package should have arrived at my house on either the fifteenth or sixteenth of May, the seventeenth at the latest.'

I jotted a few notes down in my notebook. 'I'll need to speak to your postman, I think.'

'Postwoman, on our street, actually,' said Tom. 'Postlady? Postgirl? Anyway, I've already questioned her. Our post always arrives at eleven o'clock, give or take five minutes. I was waiting for her this morning and asked her if she remembered bringing a package for me.'

'And did she?'

'Yes.'

'Ah! When?'

'She can't remember.'

'Bum.'

'She says she brought the package, but nobody was in, and she left one of those card thingies, that says: *We tried to deliver a parcel, but you were out, and now you'll have to come and fetch it yourself*, you know?'

'Yes, I've seen them. Like a postcard. I take it there's no card tucked out of sight under your doormat or anything?'

'No way. I've searched. Twice,' said Tom.

At this point, I could see three distinct alternatives. There were three possibilities relating to the fate of the parcel and/or the postcard.

Can you work out what they were?

Possibility 1: The postwoman was mistaken and the parcel was simply delivered to the wrong address, this mysterious kid's address.

Possibility 2: The postwoman was telling the truth and the parcel was picked up by someone else from the post sorting office.

Possibility 3: The postwoman was telling the truth, and the card she left was picked up by someone outside Tom's household and used to collect the parcel.

'OK,' I said, 'let's see now . . . On the days you would have expected the package to arrive, was there someone at your house?'

'Yes, without the faintest shadow of a doubt,' said Tom. 'Both my parents were at home on the fifteenth and sixteenth, and all three of us were there on the seventeenth. It was a Saturday.'

'And what if the package arrived after those dates? If it arrived later than expected?'

'There would *still* be someone at home. I guarantee it.'

This implied that Possibility 1 was the most likely.

'Who else is there at home? Could someone have collected that package and then forgotten about it?' I said.

'There's only my parents,' said Tom. 'And there's no way they'd have forgotten. I've asked them about it again and again and again. And again.'

This implied that either Possibility 1 or Possibility 3

were the most likely. So, on balance, it looked like the postwoman was telling porkies. Or had a defective memory.

But . . . were we *really* looking at a simple coincidence here? *Could* the parcel have been accidentally delivered to another kid, who spotted the mistake and decided to take advantage of it? That was a question which couldn't be answered unless I could track this kid down!

'I suppose it's also possible,' I said, 'that the radio station could have made the mistake. Perhaps you didn't win after all. Maybe the DJ called the wrong number.'

'What, he meant to call *another* Tom Bland? Who'd *also* entered the same competition?'

'Weird coincidences do happen,' I said. 'Believe me, I've come across some pretty eye-popping ones in my time.'

'No,' said Tom, folding his arms crossly. 'When he originally called, he checked my address, to make sure he'd send the package to the right place.'

'Ah,' I said. 'I can see that this business is going to be more complex that it first appears. Can I keep this newspaper page?'

'Please do,' sniffed Tom. 'If I have to look at those smug faces for one more minute I think I'll vomit.'

'I'll report back to you as soon as I can. In the meantime, I need to think.'

A Page From My Notebook

Everything turns on the real identity of this 'other' Tom Bland. (Assuming, that is, that his real name isn't Tom Bland!)

Priority 1: Identify the imposter.

Priority 2: Listen to that *Theatre Review* show the imposter appeared on. This could contain important clues. Will get **Izzy** on the case!

There are still a lot of questions floating around in my head.

Is this a set up? Is someone playing a trick on Tom? He's not exactly the most popular person at school! No, probably not - it's all rather too elaborate for a practical joke. Isn't it?

Looking back at my three Possibilities, No 1 stands out so far, but WHY would the postwoman be sure she'd had the parcel if she hadn't? It doesn't make any sense for her to LIE, she'd have nothing to gain. No, I think Possibility 3 is the likely one.

But if someone DID steal that postcard, then (once again!) WHY? If you saw a delivery card sitting there, you'd have no idea what the delivery WAS. It might be a garden gnome, or a pile of dirty underwear, or something else you wouldn't want in a million years. Would you really steal the card without knowing what you'd end up with? WAIT! Unless, somehow, the one who nicked the card DID know about the package's contents? A-HA! Now THAT makes sense! Should check this with Tom tomorrow.

CHAPTER THREE

FOLLOWING THE ADVICE OF MY notebook, I went to find Tom at school the next morning. He was pinning a small poster to the noticeboard, advertising a show he was in at a local amateur dramatics club.

'That competition entry of yours,' I said. 'Who else knew about it?'

'Apart from my parents, nobody,' said Tom, standing back to make sure the poster was up straight.

'And what about after you knew you'd won?' I said.

'Same thing,' said Tom.

'What, you've told nobody at school? No friends, relatives, neighbours? Not the people at the amateur dramatics club?'

Tom gave me a theatrical stare. 'The cultural savages

of this school wouldn't be interested, would they? And as for my fellow artistes at the club, well, they'd only be bitterly jealous. So, no, nobody . . .' (You can see why he wasn't the most popular kid in school, can't you?)

'Sorry, you'll have to excuse me,' he said, 'I've got a rehearsal for the end-of-term musical.'

And off he went. I was left feeling even more puzzled than before. So, I thought, the only other people, outside Tom and his parents, who could have known about that package were the people at the radio station. And they were the ones who were giving the prize away!

None of it made any sense. I went to find my great friend and Official Ruler of Infoland, Izzy Moustique.

'Whatcha working on?' she said.

'A strange case of stolen identity,' I said. 'Someone at this school has been impersonated by a kid he's never even seen before.' I fetched the newspaper page from my school bag.

'Who's the someone?' said Izzy.

'Tom Bland,' I said.

'Tom Bland?' said Izzy, wrinkling her nose. 'That stuck-up pig? Why didn't you tell him to go take a running jump?'

I glared at her. 'You should know me better than that. My job is to see justice done, not to judge who deserves justice.'

I think she felt suitably told off. She pulled a stretchy-mouthed face at me. I handed her the page.

'Is this the kid?' she said, unfolding the page and examining the picture.

'Yup,' I said. 'You're the best-connected person I know. I need you to circulate that photo around your social network. Someone must know that guy.'

'Okey-dokey,' said Izzy.

'One more thing,' I said. 'Can you get hold of a recording of the *Theatre Review* show on Vibe FM? The last two or three programmes should do.'

'Okey-dokey again,' said Izzy.

At that moment, the bell sounded for the next lesson. As I trudged reluctantly towards the Pit Of Doom (or 'maths' as some people call it), I was totally confident that my investigations were heading for success. Izzy's grapevine was sure to locate that kid, and Izzy's amazing research skills would soon turn up that radio show, too. Both these things would give me important clues.

As soon as school was finished for the day, I headed to the post office in the town centre, to gather up another important clue. I needed to find out who had signed for Tom's parcel.

I was hoping that – *if* the package had simply gone to the wrong house – this whoever-had-signed had put down their real name before realising that the package wasn't for them after all. (Mind you, there was *also* the possibility that whoever-had-signed actually *was* called Tom Bland, by coincidence, and that the . . .) ArRRGgh! The possible complications were starting to make my brain itch!

Let's just get a look at that signature, I thought. Whatever it says, it's an important clue. I'll deal with the complications later!

Inside the post office, I went around to the parcels collection area. Behind the chunky counter and the scratched plastic screen on top of it, were racks of battered packages wrapped in brown paper and covered in address labels and barcodes. I pressed the little buzzer on the counter marked *Press for Service* and a tiny man with big glasses appeared.

'Yes?' he said, in a voice like a cat being stepped on.

'Hello. I need to see a signature. I think a parcel might have been delivered to the wrong place, and —'

'Not possible, friend. Address on parcel, parcel delivered correctly. Mistakes not possible, friend.'

I thought for a moment or two. 'OKaaaaay,' I said. 'I think a parcel might have been delivered *correctly*, but I need to check who signed for it.'

'Not possible, friend,' said Mr Tiny Big Glasses. 'Not without completing form B451Q, Request for Delivery Information.'

'OKaaaaay,' I said. 'Do you have a copy of form B451Q, Request for Delivery Information, that I can fill in?'

'No. Post office website download only.'

'I see,' I said. 'Let's suppose I download the form, fill it in, and bring it back here. Then can I check who signed?'

'No. Apply by website only. Email reply to your application will be forwarded within twenty-one working days.'

'I see,' I said. 'But I *can* get the information after twenty-one working days, can I?'

'No. Must be eighteen years old or above.'

'I see. Would it help if I said I was a detective following up an important clue?'

'No.'

'I see,' I said. I considered the matter carefully. 'While I'm here, can I ask a question about deliveries?'

'Fire away, friend. We're here to help.' He pointed to the little badge that was pinned to his short-sleeved shirt. It said: *Here to Help*.

'OKaaaay,' I said. 'A friend of mine says he gets his mail delivered every day at exactly eleven o'clock. Would that be an accurate thing for him to say, do you suppose, at all, perhaps, maybe?'

'Yes,' he said. 'Deliveries from this office one hundred per cent timed to schedule. Failure to deliver at the specified time is not possible. Except on every third Saturday, obviously.'

'Why?' I said. 'What happens every third Saturday?'

'Training session. All deliveries timed at thirty minutes later than normal on those dates. Recent dates being June seventh, May seventeeth, April twenty-sixth.'

'I see. Well, thank you very much, and goodbye.' I stalked out of the post office grumbling under my breath.

Hmm. So. No clue there, then.

Oh well, never mind, I thought to myself. The clues that will come from Izzy's enquiries should be enough to make definite progress on this case. I decided to head for —

Wait!

I *had* been given a clue after all! I thought back to what Tom had told me about the delivery of the package. Then I remembered what that miserable twerp in the post office had told me about deliveries. A quick cross-reference gave me an important fact that Tom was unlikely to be aware of!

Can you spot it?

As far as Tom was concerned, the mail got delivered to his house at eleven *every* morning. *But* according to the miserable twerp in the post office, deliveries were half an hour later every third Saturday.

And one of those Saturdays was May seventeenth. One of the three dates on which the package could/should have arrived at Tom's house. *So . . .* if the package had arrived at Tom's on May seventeenth, it would have arrived half an hour *after* Tom expected it. He could easily have thought there was no mail that day, if he was waiting for eleven o'clock!

This new information didn't go anywhere near solving the problem of what had actually happened to the package, but it did open up some new possibilities.

I decided to head for Tom's house. I wanted to take a look at the scene of the crime. Assuming that the package *had* turned up there. Or assuming that the postwoman hadn't lied and had — *Aargh!* Brain itch again!

I was still three streets away from Tom's when I first noticed the smell. By the time I got to his front door, the smell was rather more than noticeable. In fact, it was battering at my nose like a rotting fish being stuffed up both nostrils.

Pinching my nose, I also noticed that half the street was covered in road digger's barriers and piles of earth.

'You habbig the drains dub here,' I said, blocking my nose with as many fingers as would fit up there.

'We're getting used to the pong,' said Tom sadly. 'You've just missed the workmen, they've finished for today. They've been at this for weeks. Weeks! They're digging up all the drains, all the sewerage systems, the lot. Half the houses are having their plumbing done at the same time. Including this one. It's not good enough! How can I learn my lines for the end-of-term musical when there's drilling and whopping great diggers all over the place? Disgraceful!'

'Can't they be hurried up?' I said. The whiff was starting to make my eyes water.

'That's precisely what I've asked my dad. Several dozen times a day. He takes *no* notice! I think he likes it.'

'Huh?'

'He works for the council,' said Tom, sneering with embarrassment. 'He's in charge of drainage. All the workmen are his crew. I think he's enjoying having them around to keep an eye on.'

I turned to survey the street. It was a complete mess. Enormous sections of pipe were stacked up to one side, and equally enormous drums of cable were stacked up on the other.

'Have these workmen been in this house a lot?' I said.

'All over the place!' moaned Tom. 'For *weeks*! Every

time I try to rehearse a scene there's some deafening noise or other: boots tramping up and down, plumbers whacking holes in the walls. I'm fed up of it!'

I had a lightbulb-above-my-head moment.

Are you thinking what I was thinking?

If there were workmen in and out of the house all the time, the mystery of the missing delivery postcard now had plenty of suspects. Like the clue I'd picked up at the Post Office, this new information still didn't tell me *how* or *why* the postcard had come to be stolen, but it was another step forward.

'Do you think one of these workmen could have got hold of your parcel?' I said.

'I don't see why,' said Tom. 'They still wouldn't know what was in it, would they? And those two parents in the newspaper picture weren't anyone who works on this crew, I know that for a fact.'

Even so, this was a lead I couldn't afford to ignore. I asked Tom to write down an exact timetable of what was going on in the house on the mornings of the three crucial dates: May 15th, 16th and 17th.

'Ask whoever was around for details,' I said.

'If you insist,' said Tom.

'And as your dad's in charge of the work going on, can you get hold of a list of the people who were working here on those dates?'

'Easily,' said Tom.

I headed for home. This was partly because I was eager to find out what news there might be from Izzy, but mostly because I wanted to get away from that awful pong.

I called Izzy from the bus. I was certain she'd have come up with something.

'How's it going?' I said. 'Have you circulated the photo?'

'Yes, I've sent it to every contact in my phone's address book. And half my cousins have sent it to their contacts too. It's been seen by loads of people.'

'And?'

'Nothing.'

'*Nothing*?' I cried. Several passengers on the bus were giving me funny looks. I think the smell might have been clinging to me. 'But *someone* must know that kid.'

'Nobody around here, that's for sure,' said Izzy.

Hmm. So. No clues there, then.

'What about the radio show?' I said.

'Ah!' said Izzy. 'Vibe FM does podcasts of almost all its programmes . . .'

'Excellent!'

'The only thing is, they're not very good at updating their website. The most recent edition of *Theatre Review* they've got available is dated from the last week in March. I tried calling the station, but there's no way I can get a copy of a more recent show. The only way to hear it would be to find someone who just happened to have recorded it.'

Hmm. So. No clues there, then, either.

This was turning out to be a day full of unexpected results!

A Page From My Notebook

I am: confused, puzzled, perplexed, baffled, mystified, bemused, and several other words I've just looked up in my school thesaurus!

If that kid isn't from anywhere near here, then where IS he from? And if he's NOT local, how did he get that postcard? IS there a connection with Tom's workmen?

The timetable I've asked Tom to write down is now VITAL. I'm relying on it to give me a clear indication of how and why the card went missing. If it doesn't, this investigation is scuppered, finished, in dire straits, up the creek, etc, etc!

CHAPTER
FOUR

TOM'S TIMETABLE, WHICH HE'D COMPLETED that same evening, ran as follows:

WHAT HAPPENED AT MY HOUSE, MAY 15/ 16/ 17
by Tom Bland

Thursday 15th:
7:30 a.m. – Wake up, bathroom, dressed. Parents: downstairs – Mum preparing my packed lunch for school, Dad examining map of drainage system.
7:50 a.m. – Breakfast, all three of us in kitchen. Tell parents about my superb performance at last night's rehearsal with amateur dramatics club. Parents smile weakly, say 'That's nice, dear'. They are cultural savages.

8:15 a.m. – Workmen arrive outside. Digging begins. I run to gather up homework.

8:20 a.m. – Noise outside sounds like war zone. I leave for school, quickly.

8:30 a.m. (info from Mum) – Workmen stop for tea break. Three of them use our loo (allowed by Dad to save money on hiring building site portaloos!). They eat four packets of our biscuits ('Ooh, digestives, thanks, Mrs B!').

9:00 a.m. to 10:00 a.m. (info from Mum) – Workmen dig trench across next door's drive.

10:15 a.m. (info from Dad) – 'Lateral out-pipes re-threaded, level with drain screen flow regulators'. Thanks, Dad – means *nothing*!

10:30 a.m. (info from Mum) – Workmen stop for tea break. Five of them use our loo. They eat six packets of biscuits ('Ooh, Rich Tea, lovely, Mrs B!').

10:55 a.m. (info from Dad) – Mum goes to buy biscuits and tea.

11:00 a.m. (info from Dad) – Dad sees postwoman at other end of street.

11:35 a.m. (info from Mum) – Mum returns home. No post today.

12:00 p.m. (info from Mum) – Workmen stop for lunch.

Friday 16th:
7:30 a.m. – Wake up, bathroom, dressed. Parents:

downstairs – Mum preparing my packed lunch for school, Dad examining map of plumbing pipework for bathroom.

7:50 a.m. – Breakfast, all three of us in kitchen. Remind parents to order DVD for my birthday (*Acting in Shakespeare: A Masterclass* by Sir Gilbert Smudge). Parents sigh wearily, say, 'Yes, dear'. They are artistic knuckleheads.

8:15 a.m. – Workmen arrive outside. Digging begins. I run to gather up school bag.

8:20 a.m. – Noise outside sounds like interplanetary battle. I leave for school, even more quickly than yesterday.

8:30 a.m. (info from Mum) – Workmen stop for tea break. Seven of them use our loo. They eat nine packets of biscuits ('Ooh, custard creams, great, Mrs B!').

9:00 a.m. (info from Mum) – Man next door backs car out of driveway, rear wheels fall into trench. Man next door comes to complain about trench.

10:00 a.m. (info from Dad) – 'Discuss position of re-flow end-stops with workmen, to minimise split greasing of overhead drainage tanks'. Thanks again, Dad.

10:30 a.m. (info from Mum) – Workmen stop for tea break. Nine of them use our loo. They eat eleven packets of biscuits ('Ooh, bourbons, yummy, Mrs B!').

10:55 a.m. (info from Dad) – Mum goes to buy biscuits, tea and loo unblocker. Man from next door comes back to complain about trench some more.

11:35 a.m. (info from Mum) – Mum returns home. Finds

that three bills, two items of junk mail and a catalogue have arrived in the post today.

12:00 p.m. (info from Mum) – Workmen stop for lunch.

Saturday 17th:

8:30 a.m. – I want a lie-in. Wake up screaming due to deafening screech of drill in bathroom.

8:45 a.m. – Workmen realise they are late for tea break. There is an undignified rush for the loo. Loo broken – workmen go next door. Man from next door comes to complain about workmen using loo.

9:00 a.m. – I eat breakfast watching workmen and man from next door arguing on front lawn.

10:00 a.m. – Attempt to learn lines for end-of-term musical. Noise levels not too bad – workmen are filling in trench across next door's driveway.

10:30 a.m. – Workmen stop for tea break. Dad diverts six of them from outside work to fix our loo. Not easy – already four in bathroom doing water pipes.

11:00 a.m. – I wait at front door for post. *None!* Am outraged! Storm off.

11:15 a.m. – Water pipes workmen have finished! No more drilling! Loo fixers continue.

11:20 a.m. – Am upstairs, speaking to Mum. Radio station's parcel ought to be here by today at the latest, I tell her! *Not* good enough! *Where* is my first prize? Have to yell, due to noise outside. Meanwhile, loo fixers taking extra tea break, due to extreme difficulty of loo repairs.

11:30 a.m. – Loo fixers send one workman to buy spare part from DIY store. Noise outside now sounds like small galaxy exploding.

11:45 a.m. – Man next door backs car out of driveway, hits pile of earth where trench used to be. Workman returns with spare part.

12:00 p.m. – Workmen stop for lunch. Man next door heard weeping. Loo now fixed!

As soon as I'd read it, I could confirm something I'd already suspected. Which led me to focus on one of the three dates. Which led me to spot a clear suspect. There was one person who was in the right place at the right time to intercept that delivery postcard.

Can you see where all this was leading me?

Tom's timetable confirmed that he *had* been mistaken about the time of the postwoman's arrival on the Saturday, 17th. He thought it would arrive at 11 a.m., but I knew from my visit to the post office that it would have arrived at 11:30 a.m.

And at 11:30 a.m. on the Saturday, there was one person who was in just the right spot to see that delivery postcard dropping through the door: the workman who'd been sent to get a spare part for the broken loo!

It was now lunch break. I found Tom in the school dining hall, flipping through the script for the end-of-term musical.

'This timetable,' I said, slightly breathless from running. (I have *got* to get more exercise!) 'You mention a workman who was sent to get a spare part. What was his name?'

'No idea,' said Tom. 'They all look the same to me. Overalls, muddy boots, hair that needs a good comb . . .'

'Can you find out his name? No, no, we can't ask that, it would alert him that we're on his trail. Can you get your dad to send you a list of the six workmen who were fixing the loo? But tell him not to speak to any of those workmen about it!'

'No problem. I'll call him now.'

'And before the end of school today, I need you to write something else down for me. I've just had a brilliant idea for tracking down that mysterious kid.'

'What?' groaned Tom. 'You're getting worse than Mrs Penzler for dishing out homework!'

'Do you want this mystery solved or don't you?'

'What do you want?' he said grumpily. 'We've got half an hour before lessons.'

'Something that's right up your street. A short script! We're going to perform it at your house, after school today.'

'Script? What sort of script?' said Tom. 'How's that going to track down the kid in the photo?'

I grinned. I explained my brilliant idea, and then he grinned too.

When the end-of-school bell sounded, Tom and I were first out of the school gates. He had a bundle of handwritten pages in his blazer pocket, and we went through them as we scurried along.

'I said a short script, not a ten-part TV drama!' I protested.

'You have to establish the *scene*,' said Tom, 'and the *characters*! It must be properly played out!'

'There aren't any characters, you dollop, it's you and me talking! We just need to know what we're going to say!'

Eventually, we cut down Tom's twenty-minute stage

spectacular to a sensible length. In the end, it went like this:

T Bland: Great news, O schoolmate! I hear there are secret auditions tomorrow for a new movie!
S Smart: Movie? The glamour of Hollywood comes to our town?
T Bland: Indeed! The director is none other than Sir Gilbert Smudge, noted Shakespearean player! He seeks young persons to do all the parts, and all the backstage stuff too.
S Smart: But why?
T Bland: He is a genius. One does not question a genius. Tomorrow, five o'clock, in the park. By the crazy golf. He's keeping it secret so that flocks of useless nobodies don't turn up, like on TV talent shows. Only those with contacts in the professional theatre are getting to hear about it.
S Smart: Then why tell me?
T Bland: I don't know. Keep your mouth shut, you fool!

I wasn't at all sure that these lines were quite right, somehow. However, Tom assured me that he knew a lot more about these things that I did, and that I shouldn't question a genius.

'I called my dad,' he said, as we approached his house

and the smell of the drains started to make our teeth sweat. 'Out of the workmen who were assigned to the loo that Saturday, all but one are here today. But they go home in half an hour.'

'Then we haven't a second to lose,' I said. 'Let's hope the missing workman isn't the one we're after! Do you know your lines?'

'Of course I do!' said Tom. He showed me the list of names his dad had sent him. Each had a small photo attached, taken from the workmen's ID badges

'There's one of them, over by those pipes,' I said.

Casually, making it look as if we just happened to be passing by, we walked past the first of our suspects, playing out our little scene. I thought we did pretty well. I was almost convinced myself!

With only twenty-five minutes left, we sneaked as quickly as we could up and down the street, and in and out of Tom's house, locating the workmen in question. Luckily, we only had to play our scene four times, as two of our suspects were having a tea break. We sauntered past the kitchen, chatting as if we weren't aware that anyone was nearby, but knowing that both of them could hear us loud and clear.

If you were reading the script for the school's end-of-term musical, and not one of my case files, you'd now come to a bit which said: *New scene – the park, 5 p.m. next day. Saxby and Tom are waiting close to the crazy golf. People are passing by. Saxby and Tom are keeping a close eye on them.*

'It hasn't worked,' muttered Tom.

I glared at him. 'My brilliant ideas always work! Well, nine times out of ten. Well, seven times out of ten. Well . . . anyway, it's only just five o'clock. There's still time.'

'I knew this was a long shot,' said Tom. 'We'll never find that kid now. It's hopeless. Hopeless!'

I nudged him in the ribs, and gave a slight nod in the direction of the crazy golf course. Approaching along the tree-shaded path, looking around as if they were expecting to see a crowd, were a boy and a woman.

The same boy, and the same woman, who were in the newspaper photo.

CHAPTER FIVE

I STEPPED FORWARD. 'HELLO. YOU wouldn't be looking for the film auditions, would you?'

'Yes,' said the woman, delighted. Her voice was like a squeaky toy. 'Yes, we are, that's lucky, isn't it, Tony! We were wondering where everyone was.'

'Follow me,' I said. 'By the way, I'm Saxby, and this is Tom. Everything will be clear once we get to Tom's house, it's only on the other side of the field.'

The woman stopped looking so pleased once we got to Tom's street. That may just have been because of the awful pong. But personally, I think it had more to do with the fact that she suspected she was rumbled, and that the game was up.

'What's going on!' she said crossly. 'What are we here

for? My Tony doesn't like being messed about, do you, Tony?'

'No, Mum,' said Tony, wearily, as if he was used to merely tagging along and doing exactly what he was told.

'My Tony's going to be a big star one day, aren't you Tony.'

'Yes, Mum.'

We arrived at Tom's house, just as a tall workman with a face like an unhappy turtle emerged after his tea break. He was one of those on Tom's list, and his name was Kev. When he spotted the woman and the boy, he did a double take.

'Val!' he cried, alarmed. 'What you doin' here?'

'Who are you?' squeaked Val, doing the worst job of pretending not to know somebody I've ever seen. 'I have never seen you before in my life!'

'But, umm,' I said, 'didn't he call you? Last night? After he overheard me and Tom talking? About some top secret auditions?'

Val glared at me. She looked like an enraged squirrel. 'I told you it sounded weird!' she snarled at Kev. 'I told you they don't do auditions like that! It was a set up!'

'Aw, shut your face, Val,' said Kev. 'You're the one who wants Tony to be a celebrity.'

'Shall we all go inside and have a little chat?' I said.

'Get lost!' snapped Val. 'Come on, Tony, we're going!'

'No, Mum,' grumbled Tony. 'I've had enough of this. They've caught you, now own up to it.'

She blinked at him in bewilderment, then finally slumped at the shoulders. Flashing glances at all of us, she reluctantly stepped inside.

We all gathered in the hallway. By now, we had a small audience of other workmen, come to see what was going on with Kev. Tom's dad appeared, come to see what was going on with the other workmen.

'Tell them all how it happened, Saxby,' said Tom.

'As we all know . . . because he's gone on about it so much . . . Tom had his competition prize snatched away from under his nose. It was a simple case of four unfortunate coincidences.

'Let's go back to Saturday, May 17th. Around eleven in the morning. Tom comes down here, to this hallway, to see if the parcel he's expecting will arrive today. He waits. It doesn't turn up. He's not a happy bunny.

'But he doesn't know about Unfortunate Coincidence No 1. This is one of those one-in-three Saturdays when the local post office runs half an hour late. The post isn't due for another thirty minutes.

'He goes upstairs. He starts complaining about the situation. He has to complain loudly, because of Unfortunate Coincidence No 2. He's won this competition at a time when this whole street is being dug up, and there's constant noise from the street.

'So, Tom's moaning away, loudly, which means that the crew of six workmen in the bathroom can hear him quite clearly. He talks all about the competition, and the prize, and the parcel, and he certainly doesn't expect Unfortunate Coincidence No 3. One of the workmen who can hear every word he says is Kev over there. By coincidence, Kev knows another kid who'd love a prize like that. Or, from what I've heard, perhaps it's Val who'd appreciate it more? What is she, Kev, your sister, I'm guessing?'

Kev glanced around. Everyone was looking in his direction. He took in a long breath, let it out slowly, and gave a nod.

'Yes,' I said, 'so Kev thinks to himself: It's a pity that parcel's not on its way to Val and Tony. But then, the fourth and last of our Unfortunate Coincidences comes along. At half past eleven, Kev is sent to get some spare parts for the loo. Meanwhile, two things are happening: first, the postwoman is knocking on the door. She's got a registered parcel to deliver. Second, the noise out in the street is particularly bad. Nobody inside the house hears the postwoman knock. She assumes the family's gone out, perhaps to avoid the din. Or the smell. Anyway, she puts a delivery postcard through the letterbox.

'And at that precise moment, Kev comes down the stairs. He sees the postcard dropping on to the mat. He realises at once what that postcard is all about. And he gives in to a terrible temptation. He scoops up the card, pockets it, and sets off for the DIY store, for those spare parts, as if nothing has happened.

'Later on, he . . . I'm not sure what he did, collect the parcel and then take it to Val, or give the card to Val and let her collect the package herself?'

Everyone looked at Kev.

'Picked it up on the way home,' he mumbled at the floor. 'Just showed them the postcard.'

'Okey-dokey,' I said. 'So, he takes the parcel to Val, who lives quite a long way away.'

'How can you know where I live?' squeaked Val.

'Because we couldn't identify Tony,' I said. 'If he'd been a pupil at any school near here, we'd have found him straight away. Anyway, Kev takes the parcel to his sister Val. He explains what he's nicked. The radio station don't know the real Tom Bland, do they? All Val's got to do is take Tony and her husband along, and pretend their surname is Bland. And so that's just what they do. The radio station are none the wiser. As far as they're concerned, the prizewinner came along with his mum and dad, and has received his prize.

'However, the fake Blands didn't foresee one thing.

131

They didn't realise that the radio station would get the local paper to feature the winner. They must have had a fright when the photographer turned up. They couldn't very well refuse to have their picture taken, could they?

'Oh well, never mind. They were confident that even if the real Tom Bland saw the picture, he probably wouldn't be able to trace them. And perhaps, under other circumstances, he wouldn't. But he had Saxby Smart to call on, didn't he?'

Everyone who was crammed into the hallway started to applaud. Well, everyone except Val, Kev and Tony, that is. And me, obviously.

Tom's dad tapped Kev on the shoulder. He said he'd like a quiet word with Kev in the kitchen. Val stood there looking like a chipmunk who can't work out why the lights have gone out and then suddenly realises it's been eaten by a bear. Tony walked over to Tom. I could see Tom mentally preparing a viciously sarcastic comment.

'I'm really sorry,' said Tony. 'It wasn't my idea, honest.'

'Oh. Right,' said Tom. I could see him mentally putting his viciously sarcastic comment to one side.

'I do quite like the theatre, though,' said Tony. 'I like doing the lighting.'

'Really?' said Tom. 'The amateur dramatics club I

132

belong to needs someone to do the lighting.' Ten minutes later, you'd think they'd been best buddies for years!

Now that the mystery was solved, Tom could go back to the radio station and explain what had happened. He thought they might be embarrassed at having been conned, but no. They realised they could splash the full story all over the media and get lots more publicity out if it.

And so could Tom. He even got calls from a couple of national papers. He had a chance to go on . . . and on, and on . . . about his various stage performances. He couldn't have been more pleased.

Me, I was feeling angry. Not because of the case, but because of my shed. As soon as I returned to it, and remembered what a mess I'd left it in, I hauled everything out in a filthy temper and started again.

After a lot of work, I found yet another new way to fit everything in. Hmm, not bad, my desk and Thinking Chair had enough space, sort of. The new arrangement was OK, but as I finished and settled down to write up some notes, it all seemed rather . . . familiar.

Then it hit me. This layout was exactly the same one I'd started with, before I even decided to reorganise. I was back where I'd started. With a long sigh, I flipped open my notebook and began to write.

Case closed.

THE GHOST
AT THE
WINDOW

CHAPTER ONE

SOMETIMES, LIVING THE LIFE OF a brilliant schoolboy detective can have its drawbacks. 'Drawbacks'? No, on second thoughts, perhaps 'complications' would be a better word. Er, or possibly 'strange and unforeseen effects'?

What I mean is, sometimes the results of investigating a case can be very unexpected. Now and again a case comes along which forces me to wonder whether I should have got involved in it at all.

I once tackled a case – a case I've labelled *The Ghost at the Window* – which made me think deeply about why I'd decided to become a brilliant schoolboy detective in the first place. The end of this case left me flopped in my Thinking Chair, mulling over all sorts of horribly difficult questions, such as: 'Would it have been better if

I hadn't interfered?', and 'Have I done a *good* thing or a *bad* thing?'

I got through a whole packet of chocolate biscuits before I could even get these questions straight in my head. It's no wonder people keep telling me to cut down on the carbs!

The Ghost at the Window was a rather sad and tragic case. It began shortly after I'd had a dazzlingly stupendous idea.

For a while, I'd been trying to reorganise my garden shed so that there was more room for my detective stuff in there, next to all the gardening and DIY equipment I'm forced to share the shed with. You'd think that a job like that would be quite easy, wouldn't you? Wrong. It was driving me absolutely *mad*!

Each time I took everything *out* of the shed, and then put it *back*, I seemed to end up with more boxes of this 'n' that than I started with. I was starting to believe that the lawnmower and the old paint tins had invited a load of friends over, just to annoy me! This was a *simple* matter or reorganising things: *why* did it keep going *wrong*?

And then I had that dazzlingly stupendous idea I just mentioned. If, I thought to myself, I can't stack all this rubbish up without leaving myself less than four square centimetres of space, then why not simply *step over* the problem? A-ha, all I've got to do is lay down the gardening and DIY stuff in a layer across the shed floor. Then my desk, my filing cabinet of case notes and my Thinking Chair can all sit *on top*. I'll even have room to pace up and down in! Now *that* is a dazzlingly stupendous idea!

Unfortunately . . .

By the time I'd finished, I'd realised that it wasn't quite such a clever zap of inspiration after all. My desk, case notes and Thinking Chair were all lurching at peculiar angles. I couldn't take more than a step or two before getting my foot wedged in a plant pot or caught up in the garden hose.

I shut my eyes and sighed, sliding my hands down the sides of my face in despair.

And then there was a gentle knock at the shed door. A voice called, 'Anyone home?'

'Come in!' I cried.

The door was opened by Jennifer Bell, a girl in my class at school. She was a big girl, with rosy cheeks and prominent features. Her dark hair was sliced into a sharply defined bob, and the legs of her jeans were tucked into a pair of green wellies.

'Hi, Jen!' I said.

She looked at the layer of debris on the shed floor. 'Oh, should I stay out here?'

'No, no, come on in. Just tread on stuff. Sorry about

the mess. I'm reorganising. Not quite finished yet.'

She crunched over the lawnmower flex. I indicated for her to sit in my Thinking Chair while I hopped on to the desk.

I often perch on the desk when talking to clients. It allows me the chance to strike thoughtful, detective-like poses, if necessary.

'Oh,' I said, 'I didn't know you help out at the Wild Rabbit Sanctuary.'

'Yes. I've . . . Hang on, how can you possibly know that?' she asked.

'Your wellies,' I said. 'It's a warm, dry day. The only place I can think of around here where you'd need to wear wellies is the Wild Rabbit Sanctuary.'

'How do you know I wasn't just visiting?' she said.

'A visitor wouldn't have got those little bits of straw stuck to their jeans. You've been cleaning out the hutches. Now then, how can I help you?'

She paused for a moment, almost as if she was reluctant to continue. 'Have you heard of a thief nicknamed Pat the Hat?'

'Hah! You bet I have!' I cried.

A Bit of Background Info: About ten or eleven or so years ago, Pat the Hat (or the Mad Hatter as the media called him before his identity was known), was a criminal based in London. He chose his targets with great care, and when he struck it was with breathtaking nerve and ingenuity.

He worked out amazingly clever schemes for robbing banks, jewellers, all sorts. He once conned a supermarket into letting him drive away with a lorryload of TVs, by making them think he was an undercover cop and that the TVs were stolen! His schemes were both brilliantly simple and brilliantly executed. If it wasn't for the fact that he was a common thief who was simply *stealing* from people, you could almost admire his sheer guts!

He got his nickname from the way he'd leave a little, neatly folded paper hat at the scene of each crime. I mean, this guy was just stringing the police along and having a laugh! There'd often be cheeky notes written inside the hats: *Here's a clue – I got in through the sewers*, that sort of thing.

Those hats were the only way the police even knew that these robberies had been done by the same man. He was, as they say, a master of disguise – he created a whole new identity for every job.

What's more, he was never caught. For two reasons: 1) he made a clean getaway every single time, and 2) after several years on the Most Wanted lists, he was killed during a high-speed chase with detectives from Scotland Yard. He'd been hired by a gang who wanted to rob a security van carrying millions of pounds in cash. He double-crossed the gang and ran off with the loot. A couple of days later the police got an anonymous phone call (obviously from one of the boiling-mad gang members!) telling them the Mad Hatter's real name (Patrick Bell, as it turned out).

The chase was on. Pat the Hat managed to get as far as the south coast of France before the cops cornered him! At a hundred and ten miles per hour, his car skidded, went off a cliff and hit the rocks below.

'Oh yes,' I said. 'I've definitely heard of Pat the Hat. What's he to do with you?'

Jennifer looked at me glumly. 'And there was me thinking you were a great detective! Do you really need me to tell you?'

I crumpled my brow. Umm . . .

Have you spotted what I hadn't?

'Of course!' I cried, snapping my fingers. 'His surname was Bell, and so is yours. Sorry, you're right, I should have spotted that one. What was he, your uncle?'

'No,' said Jennifer, 'Pat the Hat was my father. I was barely a toddler when he died. I don't remember him at all.'

'But what brings you here today?' I said. 'His death was more than a decade ago.'

'I can trust you, can't I?' said Jennifer in a low voice.

'Of course,' I said seriously.

'A couple of days ago, the police came to see my mother and me,' said Jennifer. 'They told us that the day before, the Steadfast & Permanent Building Society up in town had been robbed. The thief had simply walked in, disguised as the Head of Accounting. He hacked into the office computer, then transferred seven hundred thousand pounds out of various bank accounts into an untraceable account overseas somewhere. On top of that, he opened the safe in the Head of Accounting's office and made off with another twenty thousand in cash.'

I almost gasped in amazement. 'This Head of Accounting. He's very fat, right? They think the thief hid the cash inside the fake stomach that was part of his disguise?'

'Yes.'

'Hah!' I cried, clapping my hands together. 'That's

exactly what Pat the Hat did, oooh, where was it? Some big bank in the City of London. He dressed up as the most unpopular bloke in the office. Nobody took a second look at him! Genius! Er, well, y'know, *evil* genius, obviously.'

From the stern look on Jennifer's face, I realised it was time to stop looking so gleefully interested in Pat the Hat and start looking more sensitive and concerned instead.

'The police said that this crime followed every last detail of what my father did,' said Jennifer. 'There was even a paper hat left in the safe. Inside, the words *Greetings from a dead man* were written in what looked like my father's handwriting. The police said it was as if my father had risen up out of his grave, and was re-starting his career in crime. As a ghost!'

CHAPTER
TWO

'WHY HASN'T THIS BEEN ALL over the news?' I asked. 'It'd be front page stuff – nothing like that's happened around here for ages.'

'The police are trying to keep it quiet as long as possible,' said Jennifer. 'They say they want time to investigate without the press looking over their shoulders. Even so, they reckon it'll hit the papers in a day or two.'

'Have they got no clues so far?' I asked. 'After all, it's a pretty startling coincidence, this Pat the Hat robbery taking place in the same town where Pat the Hat's family just *happen* to be living.'

'They say they've got nothing,' said Jennifer. 'And the coincidence is more than startling, it's frightening. I think *that's* why the police came to talk to my mother and me. But they're clutching at straws. They wanted to know if my mother could remember anything from the old days which might give them a lead.'

'I, umm, don't want to ask an insensitive question,' I said, carefully, 'but all those years ago, when Pat the Hat was committing his original crimes, didn't your mum know what was going on?'

'No,' said Jennifer. 'He fooled her every bit as much as he fooled the rest of the world. Believe it or not, she thought he had a well-paid job . . . in a bank! He'd leave the house every morning, research his next robbery, then come home at night pretending he'd spent the day in business meetings. At the time, my mother had a job which involved a lot of travelling, so it wasn't hard for him to maintain his cover story.'

I almost chuckled 'genius' again. But I didn't. (Think sensitive and concerned, you fool!)

'Well,' said Jennifer, 'she knew right at the end, but by then it was too late.'

'At the end?'

'When he double-crossed that gang who'd hired him. He realised he'd have to lay low for a while, go somewhere where he couldn't be traced, because the gang were out for blood. And laying low would blow his cover. So he told my mother everything. But that night the gang gave the police his name, as revenge. He went on the run and then a few days later he was dead. The police questioned my mother but they soon realised she was totally shocked by what he'd told her and that she hadn't been involved in his crimes.'

It occurred to me that there were really only two possibilities that I needed to consider here. That is, two possibilities about *who* was responsible for the robbery a few days ago.

They amounted to a simple logical choice. Have you spotted them?

Possibility No 1: Could Pat the Hat be alive?

'Have, umm,' I began, not quite knowing how to put the question without, you know, touching a bit of a raw nerve, or, maybe, you know, asking something that . . . Oh, just *ask* the bloomin' question!

'Have you considered the possibility that your dad is still alive?' I said. 'Could he have escaped from that crash?'

'We've been considering it non-stop,' said Jennifer. 'The thought has been upsetting my mother terribly. All this has brought back a lot of horrible memories for her. That's the reason we moved out of London years ago and came here. To escape the past. She still misses him a lot and she says she still loves him.'

'I take it, then, that it's a possibility you've dismissed?' I said.

'When his car went off that cliff,' said Jennifer, 'it dropped almost fifty metres. It hit rock at over a hundred miles an hour and exploded so hard that all that was left were scraps of metal. The police found DNA traces in the wreckage. They even found the two tiny diamonds he'd had specially embedded into his gold wedding ring. My mother said those diamonds were supposed to symbolise the two of them, him and her. No, he's definitely dead. DNA evidence can't be faked.'

'Yes, that's true,' I said.

So . . .

Possibility No 2: Someone is imitating Pat the Hat's crimes.

'It's the only explanation,' I said.

'Right,' said Jennifer. 'And it's why I've come to see you.'

I frowned. 'How do you mean?'

Jennifer leaned forward on the Thinking Chair. The gardening stuff beneath the chair creaked and shifted. 'I think I know who did it,' she said. 'The robbery.'

'You do?' I cried.

'That's what I need your help on. I need you to help me catch him.'

'So, who is it?' I asked.

'One of my next-door neighbours,' said Jennifer. 'A guy called Henry Westwick. I've noticed that —'

'Waitwaitwait,' I interrupted. 'Your *neighbour*?'

'Yes,' said Jennifer. 'Another startling coincidence, right?'

'You're telling me!' I cried. 'Has he got any reason to dislike you or your mum?'

'No, we get on fine.'

'But, he knows about the connection between you and Pat the Hat, yes?'

'No,' said Jennifer. 'It's not a *secret*, but neither Mum nor I ever talk about it.'

(I frowned. This coincidence stuff was zooming past

'startling' and heading straight for 'incredible'! I decided to put the matter to the back of my mind, and give it some more thought later.)

'If the police are doing this all-out investigation,' I said, 'shouldn't you go to *them* with this? I mean, obviously, having a brilliant schoolboy detective like me on the case will get things sorted out much quicker, but even so . . . Surely they need to know first?'

Jennifer shook her head abruptly. She'd obviously thought hard about this, and she'd come to a firm decision. 'No. This is personal. My mother's upset, I'm upset; it's as if this guy is laughing in our faces, as if he doesn't care who he's hurting by copying Pat the Hat. I want to sort him out myself. I want to be able to hand the man responsible over to the police personally. I want to give them proof.'

'So, you can't actually prove that this Henry Westwick is guilty?' I said.

'Not yet. That's where you come in,' said Jennifer.

'What makes you so sure he did it?' I said.

'Henry Westwick works at the college in town. He's a teacher. He lectures in psychology, the human mind, human behaviour, that sort of thing. He's an absolute nut about crime and criminals. He's even worse than you!'

'Er, thanks,' I muttered.

'I've been doing some detective work of my own. He's been missing classes. I know because my friend's sister's boyfriend is on the course he teaches. I asked around. One of those missed classes coincides *exactly* with the time of the robbery. Plus, he's been lying to his family about where he's been going during these absences —'

'How —'

'I'll explain later. Plus, he has a grudge against that building society he robbed, the Head of Accounting in particular. He hates that man! *And* there are other people in my street I think he might target —'

'How —'

'I'll explain later. He had the motive, the opportunity, and the method. Those are the things *you're* always talking about in terms of suspects, aren't they? The only problem is, I don't have the *proof*. I need *you*!'

'Saxby Smart is on the case!' I grinned. 'Go home, keep a close eye on our suspect, and I'll come over to see you later on. If you're right, we haven't a moment to lose. Pat the Hat struck when least expected, so we can assume his imitator will do the same. He might be planning another crime right now.'

My mind was still reeling from the sheer oddity of it all, but I quickly reminded myself that my job was to find answers. As soon as Jennifer had gone, I got on the phone to my great friend Isobel 'Izzy' Moustique, that Mistress of All Data. I asked her to dig around for anything she could find on the Mad Hatter. If this Henry Westwick was setting himself up as Pat the Hat Mark 2, it was vital that I know as much about the original as possible.

The hunt was on!

A Page From My Notebook

Here's a newspaper cutting Izzy found, dated 22nd August, eleven years ago:

END OF THE ROAD FOR MAD HATTER

. . . Detectives from Scotland Yard, in co-operation with the French police force, pursued the Mad Hatter as he fled south of the town of Avignon along the River Rhone. The thief, who is now said to be the mysterious fifth gang member in the recent Knightsbridge security van robbery, lost control of his car. It fell into a narrow rock gully along the river valley and was completely destroyed when the petrol tank exploded. Forensic experts are still at the scene, but unofficial sources have confirmed that DNA traces from the Mad Hatter have been recovered from the crash, along with small fragments of bone and a wedding ring which could not be removed from Bell's finger, as the knuckle above it had become too large . . .'

And here's another, from a different newspaper, published on the same date:

HATTER'S ESCAPE ENDS IN DEATH

... The Mad Hatter's identity – now known to have been Patrick William Bell – was supplied to police in a phone call made at 11:33 p.m. three days ago, 19 August. A team of officers immediately moved in on Bell's address, but he evaded them at the last minute, abandoning his wife and young daughter. In disguise, he crossed the Channel to Calais by ferry, but was spotted – while swapping fake identities – by an English tourist who had seen pictures of Bell on the TV news on the morning of 18 August ...

Oddity 1: How to account for all the startling coincidences? SURELY the appearance of a Pat the Hat imitator RIGHT HERE is linked to the fact that Jennifer and her mum live RIGHT HERE? Has SOMEONE discovered the truth about them? And if so, WHY would that inspire a Pat the Hat imitator?

Oddity 2: As Jennifer said, this Henry Westwick ticks all the boxes in terms of motive, opportunity and method. But WHY would someone like that turn to crime? Sure, he's INTERESTED in the subject, and yes, he apparently has a grudge against that building society, but . . . Why would that lead him to such an EXTREME? After all, reading ghost stories doesn't turn you INTO a ghost! So WHY turn to crime? There's something I'm missing here.

Sudden thought – Henry studies crime, so he'll already know about Pat the Hat. Could it be that HE'S found out the truth about Jennifer and her mum, through his studies?

Oddity 3 (this one's an oddity from the past): Pat the Hat's robberies were planned down to the last detail. So that was a strange mistake for him to make: allowing the gang to know his real name. When he double-crossed them, they could put the cops on his tail at once! Or . . .? Could it be that he didn't INTEND to double-cross them? Is there more to the story than I think? There's something ELSE I'm missing here!

CHAPTER THREE

MAPLE GROVE HAD NOT ONE single trace of a maple tree in it, so why it was called Maple Grove I have no idea. (There's also a Hill Street in town which is about as level as you can get, and a Farmer's Walk which is about as far away from the countryside as you can get. Just one of those things, I suppose.)

Anyway, Jennifer lived at number four. There were only seven houses in Maple Grove, which formed a sort of sticky-out bit about halfway along the wide, twisting road that led from a cluster of shops to the park. The houses all looked different, and were arranged in a not-quite-lined-up pattern, with three on each side and one at the end, all of them surrounded by well-kept lawns and driveways.

Number four was the middle house on the right-hand side. As I approached, Jennifer appeared through a tall wooden gate which led to the back of the house, wheeling a bicycle along and carrying a small toolbox.

'Hi!' she called, loudly. 'Can you help me mend my bike? The brakes keep sticking!'

She swung it upside down, to rest on its handlebars and saddle. I crouched down and peered at it.

'You're asking the wrong person,' I muttered. 'Now, if you go and see my friend Muddy —'

'Shh!' she hissed. She dropped her voice to a whisper. 'There's nothing wrong with it. This is cover, so I can point out the neighbours to you without them suspecting anything.'

'Oh, right!' I said. 'Er, yeah, just what I was about to suggest. Good idea.'

We sat ourselves down on the tarmac drive that fronted the house, one of us on each side of the bike. We pretended to get busy with spanners and a hammer.

'Is this how you mend brakes?' she whispered. 'We ought to look like we're doing a proper job.'

'I haven't the faintest idea,' I shrugged. 'Give me the low-down on Maple Grove, then.'

As we talked, a breeze began to swirl around us, and someone at number seven came out and started mowing the grass on his front garden. I pulled my notebook out

of my pocket and drew a sketch map to help me keep
track of everything. This is what it looked like:

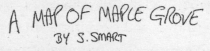

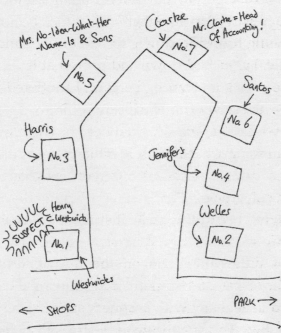

'The Westwicks are at number one, over there on the
opposite corner,' said Jennifer. 'Henry Westwick you
know about, Mrs Westwick works for a travel company,
I'm not sure where. They have two teenage daughters,
but I don't know which school they go to.'

'Obviously not St Egbert's, anyway,' I muttered.

'No. Next door to us, on the left, at number two, are the Welleses. Mr and Mrs Welles have a shop up in town, which sells really expensive laptops and top-of-the-range phones.'

'A possible target for the next robbery,' I said.

'Exactly,' said Jennifer. 'Henry Westwick is more than familiar with their set up.'

'How come?'

'Because of the Harrises,' said Jennifer, nodding slightly towards number three across the road. 'They're the family everyone knows around here. They're always having parties and barbecues, and they always invite the whole street along. These get-togethers are the centre of all the local gossip. That's how I know that Henry Westwick has been lying to his family about where he's been going recently: Mrs Westwick's been saying how busy he is at the college, but when I've cross-referenced with my friend's sister's boyfriend, those are the precise times he's been away from his job.'

'Ah!' I said. 'I take it those parties are also where you found out he hates that building society's Head of Accounting?'

'Right,' said Jennifer. 'That Head of Accounting is Mr Clarke. He and his wife live over at the end house, number seven, with their collection of antique clocks and a yappy little mutt called Billy. Repulsive creature.

And the dog's no better.'

'That's him mowing his lawn over there, is it?' I said, taking a good look at the guy through the spinning spokes of the bike's front wheel.

'Yup.'

He was the shape of an orange, with tiny little spectacles which seemed to have been embedded into his face. He scuttled his mower back and forth over his front garden with quick, precise movements. He looked like the sort of person you'd expect to see in a war film, questioning prisoners in smelly underground bunkers.

'I think you should talk to him,' said Jennifer. 'Maybe get some clues about the robbery?'

'I don't think so,' I said.

'Ah. You don't think it's necessary?'

'No, all that cut grass will set off my hay fever,' I said. 'What did he do to annoy Henry Westwick, then?'

'Mr Westwick went to the building society for a loan to buy a car. Mr Clarke there turned him down, because he'd forgotten to put the date on his application form.'

'You're kidding,' I said.

'No,' said Jennifer, shaking her head slowly. 'Mr Clarke said that if Mr Westwick couldn't fill in a form correctly then he couldn't be trusted to make his loan repayments.'

'No wonder Westwick can't stand him,' I chuckled. 'I assume he was out of the way at the time of the robbery?'

'Yes, the police said he was tricked into thinking there was a meeting at Head Office. It's caused him huge embarrassment.'

'Which will be a big bonus, as far as Henry Westwick is concerned,' I said. 'So, apart from the Welleses, is there anyone else here Westwick could target?'

'Well, not the Harris family,' said Jennifer. 'They never seem to have a penny to spare. Nice people, although the three kids are a bit bratty. They're aged seven, six, and four. Also not St Egbert's pupils.'

'What about the people in the last two houses? Numbers five and six?'

'The people in number five are a *definite* possibility,' said Jennifer. 'There's an older lady who lives there with her two grown-up sons. I have no idea what her name is. But everyone around here is sure they're into some dodgy buying and selling. People turn up at that house late at night, vans get loaded and unloaded from their garage. They're into something crooked.'

An old man came tottering around the corner from the direction of the shops. Large canvas bags overloaded with groceries hung from each hand.

'Has anybody talked to them at the Harrises' parties?' I said.

'They're the only people in the street who don't go,' said Jennifer. 'They're very secretive. You get an

160

occasional "hello" out of them, but that's about it. They're a weird lot. Their back garden is an absolute tip, too.'

This was very interesting. If Jennifer was right, the people at number seven could easily be a link between Henry Westwick and the criminal underworld. And since Westwick was knowledgeable about that sort of thing, he'd have no trouble finding a way to enlist their help. *If* he needed it, that was!

'Ah, perfect timing,' said Jennifer, waving to the approaching old man. 'This is Mr Santos. He lives at number six, next door.'

She called out a greeting and he nodded back at her with a smile. He was a frail-looking guy, with thinning grey hair and heavily framed glasses. He looked as if a strong gust of wind would topple him over, but there was a rosy glow in his cheeks. The chunky grey moustache below his big nose was so expertly clipped it appeared to be standing to attention.

'*Hola*, Jennifer,' he said, in a cracked voice which had a thick Spanish accent. 'Bike trouble?' He drew level with us and stopped.

'Yeah,' said Jennifer. 'My friend Saxby here is helping me fix it.'

Mr Santos grinned at me, casually hopped both his shopping bags into one hand and extended the other towards me. 'Glad to meet you, Saxby.'

'Hi,' I said, smiling. As I shook his hand, something felt a bit odd. I couldn't quite work out what it was, at first.

'How are you, then, Mr Santos?' said Jennifer.

'Not so bad, not so bad,' he said. 'You hear 'bout that terrible landslide in South America?'

'Yes, it was on the news,' said Jennifer.

'Mr Harris over the road told me 'bout it,' said Mr Santos, shaking his head. 'This week we think we have it bad, what with food prices going up and robbery in town and the discount shoe shop closing. But we're very lucky, in some ways, eh?'

'I guess you're right,' said Jennifer.

'Be seeing you!' he called cheerily. He tottered on his way.

'Nice old bloke,' whispered Jennifer, as he fished for his keys in his cardigan pocket and unlocked his front door. 'Reserved, though. Keeps himself to himself most of the time.'

'He's from Spain?' I said.

'Yes, he moved in here about five years ago.'

A large, dark blue car growled into the street. It glided in a wide arc and came to a stop outside number one.

Ahhhh! Here was Henry Westwick!

All four doors of the car swung open and out stepped Mrs Westwick, Daughter Westwick one, Daughter Westwick two, and finally Henry himself. If I was feeling

162

generous, I'd describe Mrs Westwick as being a woman of unconventional looks. If I was feeling cruel, I'd describe her as a bit of a fright. The gene pool had not been kind to Mrs Westwick.

Henry Westwick, on the other hand, reminded me of those marble statues you see of Roman Emperors in echoey museums. His stern, bird-like face sat on top of a wiry body which seemed to move from one elongated pose to another. There were leather patches on the elbows of his jacket and his shoes were the sort of scuffed, thick-soled footwear that looked as if it had been designed inside-out.

His two daughters were the spitting image of their mother. The four of them trooped into the house without so much as glancing at each other.

'So, that's him,' said Jennifer.

'And you're sure he doesn't know about your connection with Pat the Hat?'

'When my mother realised Henry Westwick was interested in criminology, she made doubly sure she kept her mouth shut when he was around. I tell you, if he knew, he'd never stop pestering her with questions.'

I wasn't convinced. I was *sure* that our Pat the Hat imitator must have discovered the connection. Otherwise, there were simply too many loose threads left dangling!

'Have the Westwicks lived here long?' I said.

'Oh, yes, as long as I can remember,' said Jennifer. 'In fact, Mr Santos moving in five years ago was the only change there's been in this street for ten years.'

Suddenly, I realised why Mr Santos's handshake had felt odd. I turned to Jennifer.

'Has he got half his fingers missing?'

'Er, yes, well one, I think,' said Jennifer, surprised at the question. 'And half his right foot, so he says. And a kneecap. And there are metal plates in his legs. He was caught up in some civil war in Africa about forty years ago, apparently. He was an engineer, he used to build apartment blocks all over the world.'

Jennifer's mum appeared at their front door. I'd seen her once or twice at school events and she always struck me as the type of person who could get overlooked in an otherwise empty room. She had an open, kindly face, the sort you'd look at and think: I know you from somewhere, but I can't remember your name.

'Do you two want something to eat?' she chirped.

'Oooh, yes please,' I said. 'Got anything chocolatey?'

A couple of minutes later, Jennifer's mum was in the kitchen, and Jennifer and I were hovering by the bay window in the living room, watching the street, keeping an eye on Henry Westwick's house. Mrs Westwick and her daughters reappeared and walked out of sight.

'What's the next move?' asked Jennifer.

'Hmm. Not sure,' I said, gazing out of the window. 'If we were the police, we could mount a twenty-four-hour surveillance operation and keep watch on him. But we aren't. So we can't.'

Suddenly, Jennifer and I both spun around at the sound of her mum's voice. 'This is a matter for the police,' she said. 'Let them handle it.'

'How long have you been there?' cried Jennifer.

I tried to hide the fact that I'd nearly jumped with fright. 'I didn't realise you knew what we were up to,' I said.

'I didn't,' said Jennifer's mum. 'But I know my daughter. And I've been having suspicions about Henry Westwick myself. But you can't start —'

'Yes, we can, Mother!' cried Jennifer. 'This should be down to *us*. It's for *us* to sort out!'

'No! It isn't!' insisted her mum. 'You know how upsetting this business has been, for you as well as me. I don't want you getting involved!'

I let them carry on, not quite knowing what to say. As they argued, my phone bleeped. Izzy had sent me a link to a third nespaper article. Normally, I'd have put it away and read it later, but at that moment, I was grateful for the distraction.

The article was dated 18th August, eleven years ago. It said:

KNIGHTSBRIDGE VAN GANG CAUGHT
Four Charged with Theft – Fifth Member Eludes Police

. . . All but one of the robbers responsible for last week's theft of two million pounds in cash from a London security van are now in police custody. The crooks – named as Bob Butcher, Joanne 'Knuckles' Wilson, Fred Edwards and Harry 'Stinks' Milan – were arrested as a result of police detective work. None of the money has yet been recovered. Police suspect that there was a fifth member of the gang, who has double-crossed the others and escaped with the stolen cash. However, the only name given to the police by the gang has turned out to be a fake ID, and the whereabouts of the fifth gang member remains a mystery.

As soon as I'd read it, an unexpected truth smacked me between the eyes. I was astonished.

There were certain details of Pat the Hat's story that were different from the version I'd heard so far. I could now *name* the person who'd made that phone call to the police, the call which gave the police his real name.

Look back through the newspaper articles and think about what Jennifer had told me. Can you name the caller?

'Mother, you've got to give Saxby a chance,' cried Jennifer. 'Please, just until news of the robbery hits the headlines. Saxby's brilliant at this sort of thing.'

Her mum stared blankly at me.

'No, honestly, I am,' I assured her. 'I've worked out that it was you who called the police all those years ago, and told them who the Mad Hatter really was. You haven't quite told Jennifer the truth, have you?'

The moment the words left my mouth, I knew I'd made a mistake. Something changed in the room, some unseen, unheard, untouchable something. I'd just trodden all over their memories and emotions in a horribly clumsy way. I hadn't meant to, honestly. I felt terrible.

Now it was Jennifer's turn to stare blankly at me. 'What?' she said at last. '*What*?' She turned to her mum. 'Is this true? Mum?'

'I see what you mean about him, Jennifer,' said her mum sadly. 'Perhaps I was hasty. Perhaps I should give him a chance after all.'

'Is this true?' cried Jennifer. 'Did you turn him over to the police? Did you?'

Her mum's silence gave Jennifer her answer. With a shriek of horror, Jennifer ran out of the room. Her footsteps thudded up the stairs. A door slammed.

(Article three was dated *before* the phone call. The

gang was already under lock and key when the call was made, and anyway, from this third clipping it was clear that they *didn't* know Pat the Hat's real name after all. There was only one person – other than Pat the Hat himself – who knew who he was, at 11:33 p.m., on August the nineteenth.)

'I was just so shocked,' said her mum quietly. 'He'd lied so much. And when he died, I felt it was all my fault. I've never stopped feeling guilty. I soon wished I'd never made that call. I couldn't tell Jennifer the truth. I just couldn't.'

'I'm . . . really really sorry,' I stammered. I'd never been so embarrassed and ashamed of myself in my entire life.

I turned back to the window. Mr Clarke at number seven had finished his lawn and was dumping the cuttings into a green recycling bin. Over at number one, Henry Westwick was hurrying out of his house, carrying . . .

Hang on. What was that he was carrying? A large, thin, floppy sort of case-thing. What was it? It was one of those zip-up bags you put clothes in, to stop them getting dirty. Hmm, I thought, he's probably off to the dry cleaner's.

He opened the boot of his car and laid the bag flat inside. Then he fetched a hold-all and put that in the boot as well, tucking something inside it as he did so. What was that he put in the hold-all? I couldn't quite see. An electronic device of some kind?

Suddenly, a wave of hot-cold-hot-cold flooded across me. On top of the embarrassment I was already feeling, it was a pretty unpleasant sensation!

From what I knew about Pat the Hat, and about what Henry Westwick had already done, I came to an alarming conclusion. I had to act fast!

Can you work out what I was thinking?

'That stuff he's got with him!' I cried. 'That could well be a disguise! And that's probably his toolkit in the hold-all! The rest of the family are out. Now he's *on his way to his next robbery!*'

I saw him slam the boot of his car shut.

'We've got to go after him!' I cried.

Jennifer's mum shook her head. 'Sorry, the car's in for repair. And besides, I need to have a long talk with Jennifer, don't you think?'

'Er, umm, er, umm . . .'

I was hopping about like a frog on hot coals. Without thinking, I raced out into the street. Westwick's car was backing out of his driveway.

With panic gripping me like a giant octopus, I ran towards the main road. The car accelerated, indicated right, and sped away.

CHAPTER FOUR

I SAID SEVERAL THINGS I CAN'T repeat here.

Then I had a bit of luck. As Henry Westwick's car drove off, I spotted a bus pulling in at the bus stop.

If you've read the case *Curse of the Ancient Mask*, you'll know that my dad (the one whose library of crime novels I'm always looting) is a bus driver. Which means that the local bus drivers know me, especially since the time I solved *The Mystery of the Sunken Bus Depot*. (Long story, no time to tell it now!)

I ran across to the bus and leaped on board. I was already out of breath. I am *so* unfit!

'Oh, hello Saxby,' said the driver.

'Hi Frank,' I gasped. '*Follow that car!*'

'What? I can't do that! I've got a route to follow!'

'This is an emergency!' I cried. 'A major crime is about to be committed!'

'I'm sorry,' grumbled Frank, 'I've got my passengers to think of.'

I looked round. The only passenger, sitting right at the back, was a tiny little old lady with a dome of white hair. She was tucking in to a giant bag of Thai Ultra-Hot-Flavoured Crisps.

'Are we at the shops yet?' she piped up.

'Not yet, Mrs Hillard,' called Frank, checking her in his rear-view mirror.

'Pleeease,' I begged. 'The car's getting away! The man driving it is about to be involved in a robbery!'

Frank snapped his gaze to and fro between me, the rapidly disappearing car and the old lady. He sighed. 'OK, but I'm not going far off my route!'

'Brilliant! Thank you! Fast as you can, pleeeeease!'

The bus moved off with a hiss of hydraulics. It gathered speed, its engines rumbling sluggishly. Westwick's car was still in sight – just – at the far end of the road.

The old lady had moved on to a big pack of cheese-and-pickle sandwiches. I sat at the front of the bus, hands clenched tightly on the metal rail in front of me.

The car was heading into the centre of town. Westwick obviously didn't realise he was being followed, so he wasn't making any attempt to hurry. Beneath my feet, I could feel the vibrations of the bus as it shifted up a gear.

'Are we at the shops yet?' called the old lady.

'Not yet, Mrs Hillard,' called Frank.

Even though Westwick wasn't hurrying, that car was a much quicker vehicle than the bus. Several times, the car vanished from view around a corner. My heart pounded with nerves until Frank could turn the bus's huge steering wheel and the back of the car became visible again.

'Doesn't this thing go any faster?' I cried, a flash of despair zipping through my stomach.

'D'you realise how many rules I'm already breaking here?' said Frank.

'Sorry,' I mumbled. My hands were sweating. I wiped them on my sleeves. Westwick's car was pulling into a smaller road that branched off the town's main shopping street. What was his target? A bank? A safe full of valuables?

'Haven't we just passed the shops?' called the old lady. She'd finished the sandwiches and was now stuffing down a bag of jam doughnuts. For a moment I was distracted. I couldn't help thinking: Where's she putting it all? Has she got hollow legs or something?

The bus lurched sharply to the left. The tyres gave a screech. Up ahead, the car was making its way between the tall buildings of Hanover Street. Then it turned left, on to a gravelly path, and under a gate-like barrier.

'I can't go any further,' said Frank.

'Pleeeeeeease,' I cried.

'No, I really can't. The bus is too tall, I'll hit that barrier!'

'Oh. Right,' I said.

The bus rolled up a little way short of the gravelly path, and hissed to a bouncing halt.

'Thank you so much,' I said, leaping through the doors the second they flapped open. 'See ya!'

'Are we at the shops now?' called the old lady, downing a litre of lemonade.

'Not yet, Mrs Hillard,' yelled Frank.

Once the bus had gone, I sneaked as quietly as I could along the path. Loose chippings crunched underfoot, no matter how carefully I moved. At each step, I winced.

As I reached the corner of a long, low building, I saw that the path widened out into a car park. Westwick's car was parked in the middle of a long line of vehicles.

I crouched down. I watched him unload his luggage from the boot, slinging it over his arm. The car beeped at him as he locked it and walked away.

He entered the building. The place looked dark and silent. With my nerves slowly slicing themselves to pieces, I followed him.

Inside a set of swing doors was a long, dim corridor. I could hear Westwick's footsteps echoing. The place had a vague smell to it, like old leather. Up ahead, suddenly, there was a bump. A broad rectangle of bright light lit up the corridor and I could hear an excited gaggle of voices.

I tiptoed over to where an immense curtain had been drawn back. A wide gap in the wall opened up into an enormous ballroom. People were milling about, chatting, laughing, practising dance moves. The whole place was awash with brightly coloured decorations.

'Henry, have you brought the music?' called a voice.

'I have!' called Mr Westwick. There was a ripple of relief across the room. He crossed to a table, and out of his hold-all pulled a portable hi-fi. That electronic device I'd seen in his hand was the thing's remote control.

Slowly, I turned my head and read the poster that was taped to the wall beside me: *Advanced Salsa Course – Final Exam – 7:30 p.m. – Candidates must arrive by 7 o'clock.*

Henry Westwick unzipped his clothes case, revealing a frilly, red and yellow costume. 'I'll just go and change,' he called to someone at the other end of the ballroom.

'Don't be nervous, Henry,' called the someone. 'You'll sail through it!'

Huh?

Huh?

Henry Westwick had not been on his way to commit a major crime. Henry Westwick had been on his way to a dance class.

I sneaked away.

Not only had I been an insensitive fat-head towards Jennifer and her mum, I'd *also* been totally and utterly wrong about this *entire* case!

I sneaked home, sneaked into my shed and sneaked on to my Thinking Chair. If all Henry Westwick had been doing was taking secret dance lessons, then . . . ?

Everything was buzzing around my head like a swarm of hopping-mad bees. I couldn't decide which was worse: knowing I'd caused a terrible row at Jennifer's house, or knowing my investigation of the robbery had got precisely nowhere.

And it was while I was weighing up these two awful alternatives that the big picture finally came into focus. The bees buzzed off. With a jolt of logic which almost knocked me off my chair, I suddenly spotted the truth. The *real* truth.

I could barely believe it. How could I have been so blind as not to see it straightaway? All I had to do was think back to that morning, to when Jennifer and I sat there on her driveway pretending to mend her bike. The clues had been right in front of me. Right in front of me!

How much of the truth have you pieced together?

CHAPTER
FIVE

THE FOLLOWING MORNING, IT WAS all over the news:

COPYCAT THIEF TARGETS BUILDING SOCIETY
ROBBER RAIDS STEADFAST & PERMANENT

I called Jennifer, partly to see if she was OK and partly
to ask if I could go over and talk to her and her mum. She
said it would be fine. I didn't let on that I was going to
shock her all over again.

Before I could see Jennifer, I needed to get two things
done.

First Thing: I phoned Izzy and asked her to check one
more thing for me. I needed to know what had happened
to the four original members of the gang Pat the Hat had
double-crossed. A few minutes later, she phoned back.

'Bob Butcher and Joanne "Knuckles" Wilson were released two years ago,' she said. 'They were flattened when they tried to break into an office building and used too much explosive. It fell on top of them. Fred Edwards died in prison, didn't even finish his sentence. And Harry "Stinks" Milan is also dead.'

'Recently, am I right?' I said.

'Yes. Less than a month ago. He picked a fight while he was on holiday abroad, and lost.'

'Thought so,' I said. 'That confirms my suspicions. Thanks, I'll tell you all about it later.'

Second Thing: as I arrived back at Maple Grove, I popped in to see Henry Westwick.

A short while later, I approached Jennifer's house. I could see Mr Santos, over at number six, standing in his front window. He gave me a cheery wave and I waved back. Then, I had a second thought. I took a step back and beckoned to Mr Santos. A few moments later, he emerged from his house and tottered over to me.

'Hello,' he said. 'Shelby, isn't it?'

'Saxby, yes,' I smiled. 'Sorry to disturb you, but I'm about to call on Jennifer and her mum. Could you come with me? I need, umm, a witness.'

'Witness?' said Mr Santos. 'To what?'

'You'll see in a few minutes,' I said.

Soon, the four of us were sitting on the sofas in

Jennifer's living room – me, Jennifer, Jennifer's mum, and Mr Santos. Jennifer's mum had made a pot of tea. Mr Santos sat there sipping nervously. From the way he was looking around, it suddenly occurred to me that he'd never actually been in this room before.

Everything felt a bit awkward, as if a couple of teachers had just gate-crashed your birthday party. Jennifer's mum was looking as if she'd rather be in a slime-covered cellar with a man-eating tiger than perched on her own sofa. Jennifer was giving me a look which said, 'You'd better have something important to say, 'cos you're not in my good books right now, matey.'

'Well, Saxby?' said Jennifer's mum. 'You said you'd got it all worked out?'

I wasn't at all sure how to begin. I cleared my throat.

'I'm very sorry I shocked you yesterday,' I said, eventually. 'But I'm afraid I'm about to shock you again.'

'Better finish my tea, then,' muttered Jennifer's mum without the faintest hint of humour, draining her cup.

'Well, first of all,' I said, 'I've been to see Henry Westwick this morning. He had nothing to do with the robbery. He's been taking time off from his job recently because he's been taking extra dance classes.'

'Dance classes?' said Jennifer. 'What, Henry Westwick?'

'Yes,' I said. 'He's also been going to job interviews. He'd been working towards becoming a qualified salsa dance instructor. He's grown tired of lecturing about the worst aspects of the human mind. Instead, he says he wants to, er, teach the world to boogie.'

'Henry Westwick?' spluttered Jennifer.

'Yup. He's been hiding all this from his family because he knew they'd have exactly the same reaction as you. He wanted to wait until everything was set for his change of career before he said anything. He told me that, er, they'd only rain on his parade. You should be pleased for him. He passed his final exams last night. He says he's ready to chase his dream now.'

'Is this the shock?' said Jennifer's mum.

'Er, no,' I said. 'The shock involves the person who *did* commit the robbery. You see, I know exactly who it was.'

'So, who was it?' said Jennifer.

'It was someone I'd never normally have suspected,' I said. 'But this person let something slip, yesterday.'

I glanced at Jennifer's mum. She had a steely look on her face, an unreadable expression that made me feel even more nervous than I was already.

I cleared my throat again.

'As you've probably seen,' I said, 'news of the robbery has finally hit the headlines this morning. Everyone's now going to be searching like mad for the Pat the Hat imitator. It's the only major robbery that's been reported around here for ages, but this person mentioned it yesterday, when only the police and a handful of others knew about it. It was only a brief comment, but it gave him away. Jennifer, think back to our conversation on the driveway.'

Jennifer frowned. 'But, surely, the only person you could be referring to is . . .'

'Mr Santos,' I said.

Mr Santos didn't react. The expression on his face didn't change. He gently placed his teacup on to the coffee table in front of us.

'But how . . .?' said Jennifer's mum. 'I . . . I can't believe it!'

'What?' said Jennifer. 'Nice old Mr Santos? Well, you were right, Saxby, that's certainly a shock.'

'Actually, er, that's not the shock either,' I said.

I stood up and walked over to Mr Santos. He glanced up at me. His expression still hadn't changed. His face barely moved, but somehow he told me to go ahead. He knew the game was up.

'That wasn't the shock,' I said. 'This is.'

I took hold of his grey hair, and pulled. With a snapping of hairpins, it slid off to reveal a close-cut, reddish fuzz. I took hold of his bulbous nose and pulled it away. I removed his glasses, and peeled off the rubbery appliance that altered the shape of his chin.

The teacup dropped from Jennifer's mum's hand, and

smashed on the floor. She gaped at him with a mixture of horror and disbelief, her eyes wide, her mouth shuddering in uncontrollable heartache.

'Pat?' she gasped. 'Patrick?'

'Hello,' said Patrick Bell, in a voice that was totally unlike that of Mr Santos.

Jennifer's mum screamed. Loudly. She sat back, shaky hands gripping the edge of the chair.

Jennifer slid off the sofa and leaned over the coffee table.

She gazed intently at the face of the stranger in front of her. Her lips struggled to form words, until at last she said, in a feeble whisper, 'Daddy?'

Patrick Bell smiled weakly at her. Tears welled up in his eyes. He turned to me. 'Are you goin' to tell 'em, or shall I?' he said.

'I think I can guess most of it,' I said. 'You stop me if I go wrong.'

'OK,' he nodded. He was a distinctive-looking guy, with a heavy brow and a prominent jawline. It was no wonder he'd needed to become so expert at using disguises during his criminal activities.

'You'd had several years as a highly successful thief,' I said to him, 'but the security van heist was one in a million. Divided up amongst the gang, it would net you a lot of cash. But kept all to yourself, the loot would set you up for life. You got greedy. You decided to take the risk and double-cross them.

'But pulling it off would mean revealing your secret to your wife. Even though you'd been careful not to allow the gang to know your real name, they'd still be after you. They'd stop at nothing to track you down and get revenge. So you'd need to go into hiding, to keep your wife and daughter safe as well as you.

'However, Jennifer's mum didn't take the news well. The gang had got themselves caught, and were under lock and key. You thought you had a little breathing space. But she called the police. You were forced to go on the run. Now, obviously, you weren't killed in that crash. Am I right in thinking the crash was deliberate?'

'Yeah,' said Patrick Bell. 'Scotland Yard and the French police were closing in fast. I knew I had no chance, unless they thought I was dead.'

'To convince them you were dead,' I said, 'they'd need a body. Or, if not a body, then enough evidence to convince them you'd been blown to bits. I take it you rigged the petrol tank? To make sure there'd be an explosion, and a big one at that?'

'Right,' said Patrick Bell. 'I even put a bag full of newspapers on the back seat, to make them think the money had burned up. I guess the bang was so big they couldn't find any of it.'

'I don't know how you got out of the car,' I said.

Patrick Bell smiled grimly. 'I wasn't even in it. I had the thing on a remote control. I was standing halfway up a slope, watching from above.'

'But the ring?' gasped Jennifer's mum. 'The DNA?'

'He knew he'd need some sort of proof left in the car,' I said. 'Cuttings from hair or fingernails might not be enough, and might nor survive the explosion anyway. The ring was ideal, though: it was specially made, the diamonds would certainly survive, and it was known that the ring wouldn't come off his finger. So . . .'

Jennifer whimpered, shutting her eyes.

'I snipped that finger off with a pair of gardening cutters,' said Patrick Bell, kneading his hands together as he spoke. 'It's amazing what you'll do when you're desperate. A finger and a ring wasn't much, but it would be enough to leave traces, and it'd be enough for the cops, provided they didn't look too closely. And they didn't.'

'I expect they were glad to be rid of the Mad Hatter,' I said. 'Meanwhile, Jennifer and her mum learned what had happened. Soon after, they left London and came to live here. But the rest of the story isn't clear to me. Why did you come back to England? I assume you ended up in Spain, as you took on a Spanish disguise when you came back?'

'Yeah,' said Patrick Bell. 'Once the heat was off, I

made my way south. Ended up in Barcelona. I'd taken the proceeds of the robbery with me, o' course, and I set myself up as a Mr Underhill, retired bank manager. Big house in the country, the lot. For several years, I lived it up. Parties on the beach, boats on the Mediterranean.

'But I was never happy. Not for a minute. I never realised how much I'd miss my little girl. Or her mum. I thought about them all the time. And missing them made me think about how badly I'd treated them, and how badly I'd mucked up my life.

'I could never be off guard. Not ever. The cops might work out what I'd done and come after me again. So might the gang I'd double-crossed. Even from prison they could have had me killed, if I'd been traced.

'Every time the phone rang, every time there was a knock at the door, I'd be terrified. It didn't matter how many disguises I adopted, or how many times I moved house. Someone, somehow, might catch up with me.

'It's a terrible way to live. Terrible. Back in the old days, I used to think that the danger was exciting, glamorous even. But all it does is crush you, slowly. Turns you paranoid and jumpy. It eats you from the inside. It isn't living, it's a slow, horrible death.

'I wanted to come home. I wanted to see my little girl, so badly. I was missing her growing up, her first day at school, her first loose tooth. I figured if I had to live in hiding, I could at least be in hiding near my family. So I invented Mr Santos. I could speak fluent Spanish, now I'd been in the country a few years. I could pass myself off as a foreigner back home.

'It cost me an absolute fortune. Fake IDs, untraceable vehicles, all kinds of stuff. But I got here in the end. I got the house right next door. I couldn't talk to Jennifer much, I couldn't drop the slightest hint about who I really was, I couldn't tell her how much I loved her and how sorry I was, but at least I could be near her. At least I could see her, and her mum.'

'But . . .' whispered Jennifer, wiping her eyes with a tissue, 'couldn't you have told us, in secret?'

'I couldn't take the risk,' said her father. 'If the gang ever caught up with me, that would put you in danger too. And besides, the last time I'd seen your mum, she turned me in to the cops. I had no reason to think she wouldn't do the same again. I thought she might hate me now, for what I did.'

Jennifer's mum shook her head tearfully. 'I didn't,' she whispered. 'I don't. I wouldn't have called them.'

'I didn't know that,' said Patrick Bell quietly.

'But why return to crime?' I said. 'That's the final part of the story I don't understand.'

'Believe it or not,' he said, 'the money was almost gone. I'd bought houses in Spain, even a vineyard, but I had to abandon it all when I came back here. I had to make sure I didn't leave a trail that someone could follow.

'I thought about simply getting a job. But I couldn't get a job as my real self, could I? A fake identity wouldn't stand up to the kinds of security and tax system checks you get these days. Things were looking bad – I was down to a few hundred pounds. But then, a few weeks ago, I discovered that the last member of the gang had died. Suddenly, I realised nobody would be coming to kill me any more. Suddenly, it occurred to me that Pat the Hat could return from the dead. My disguise was intact. The cops would think it was a copycat, long before they suspected the truth.

'So, I thought, one more robbery. Just one. Big enough to let me retreat into my Mr Santos disguise for ever. Mr Clarke, across the road, made a perfect target. It wasn't hard to work out how to get into that building society, not once I got talking to Mr Clarke at one of the Harrises's regular get-togethers.

'I shouldn't have left that hat, should I? But the temptation was just too great. I was too full of myself, all over again. I thought I'd leave the police baffled, and be safe and sound as nice old Mr Santos. With my pretend war wounds and my pretend accent. Perhaps I hadn't rejected my old life as much as I thought. But then I let one little detail slip, didn't I? I knew about the robbery too early. And you spotted it.'

'Yes,' I said. 'Although, it wasn't just that. The missing finger gave me the clue to what had happened eleven years ago. But that was after the clue of your shopping bags.'

'My shopping bags?'

'Yes, Mr Santos was a tottery old guy, but he shifted those bulging shopping bags around as if they were weightless. He was suspiciously stronger than he looked. I should have seen it at once, but I only started thinking about other possibilities once Henry Westwick was out of the picture. Silly of me.'

Patrick Bell, the most ingenious crook of his day, let out a long sigh and smiled at me. 'I've outwitted a lot of cops in my time, but I didn't outwit you, did I? I must be going soft in the head.'

'Soft in the head is right,' said Jennifer's mum shakily. She stood up, and suddenly dragged her not-dead-after-all husband to his feet. For a second, I thought she was going to whap him one across the face. 'You . . . stupid man!' she yelled.

Then she hugged him. Jennifer jumped up and hugged him too. I kept well out of the way.

And so ended one of the strangest cases I've ever investigated. The following day, Patrick Bell walked into the local police station and gave himself up. He'd told

Jennifer that he had to come clean, he had to stop running away and face up to what he'd done. He would go to prison, but at least she could visit him, and when he got out, he could make a new start. He could stop being terrified every time the phone rang, or someone knocked on the door, and live a better sort of life.

I returned to my shed. Something had to be done about the wretched mess I'd left it in! Well, maybe tomorrow . . .

And so, in the end, there I was, flopped in my Thinking Chair. For ages (as I said at the start of Chapter One) I was mulling over all sorts of horribly difficult questions, such as, 'Would it have been better if I hadn't interfered?', and 'Have I done a *good* thing or a *bad* thing?'

I'd solved the crime. I'd seen justice done. But I'd also turned Jennifer's life upside down. I'd forced her mum to reveal a painful secret. I'd thrown the pair of them into turmoil. Was it my fault? Could I have acted differently? I still don't know. What do you think?

After a while, and after another half a packet of chocolate biscuits, I did come to a conclusion. Sometimes, the truth is painful. But, in the end, it's usually less painful than lies. Because covering up the truth rarely does *anyone* any good.

Case closed.

Epilogue

READERS OF MY OTHER CASE FILES may be wondering where my arch enemy, that low-down rat Harry Lovecraft, has been hiding for the duration of this book. The truth is, he was keeping his head down, and his nose clean. He was plotting a terrible revenge, as you'll discover in the volume of my case files entitled *Five Seconds to Doomsday* . . .